Praise for The Last Brazil of Benjamin East

★★★★★ "Tender-hearted and provocative from beginning to end, *The Last Brazil of Benjamin East* is an engaging read and destined to be an award winner."

-- *San Francisco Book Review*

"A spirited, hopeful novel that serves as a reminder that change is always possible."

-- *Kirkus Reviews*

"The story is engaging and Benjamin is unforgettable: a complicated, and sympathetic character who captured and kept my interest. The prose is clear, smart, funny, and knowing. The insistent search for meaning shines through."

-- Robert Koppel, author of *Why Love?*

Jonathan Freedman is "a beautiful prose stylist...a very provocative writer."

-- Patricia A. O'Connell, *Commonweal*

"A big-hearted, compelling, zany, funny, fast-paced novel."

-- Sara Houghteling, author, *Pictures At An Exhibition*

D1593715

The Last Brazil

of

Benjamin East

June 27, 2015 San Francisco

To Michelle,

Delighted to meet you at ALA.

Would be proud to be considered for one of your reading lists.

Jonathan Freedman

jonathanfreedman755@gmail.com

ALSO BY
JONATHAN FREEDMAN

Collected Essays:

Pulitzer Prize-winning Editorials, San Diego Tribune

Fiction and Illustrations:

The Man Who'd Bounce the World

Stanley Scuka Bounces a Bean

Bounce

Non-Fiction:

*From Cradle to Grave: The Human Face of
Poverty in America*

*Wall of Fame: One Teacher, One Class, and the Power to
Change Schools and Transform Lives*

The Last Brazil

of

Benjamin East

A NOVEL

Jonathan Freedman

Bright Lights Press
PALO ALTO, CA

Bright Lights Press
P.O. Box 306
Palo Alto, CA 94303
www.BrightLightsPress.com

Cover Design by Yulia Zimmerman
Book Layout @2015 BookDesignTemplates.com

Publisher's Note: This is a work of fiction. Names, characters, places, and incidents are a product of the author's imagination. Locales and public names are sometimes used for atmospheric purposes. Resemblance to actual people, living or dead, or to businesses, companies, events, institutions, or locales is coincidental.

The Last Brazil of Benjamin East/ Jonathan Freedman. -- 1st ed.
ISBN: 978-1-939555-10-6 paperback
ISBN: 978-1-939555-11-3 ebook

To Isabelle
With Love & Admiration
On our Fifteenth Anniversary

To Four Generations of Family:

My parents, Betty & Marshall Freedman
My sister, Tracy & the Robins Gang
My children, Nick, Viva & Lincoln Freedman
My daughter, Madigan & son-in-law, Ethan Kent
My grandchildren, Belle & Milo

CHAPTER 1

The stars of the Southern Cross sank into the equator, leaving their imprint on the tailfin of a Brazilian jetliner descending through low clouds toward the runway of Miami International Airport.

The last passenger to deplane was an elderly American gentleman attired in a rumpled Panama hat, lavender shirt, and flowered necktie. The flight roster identified him as Benjamin East, and he was traveling alone on a one-way ticket from Rio de Janeiro. He toted a leather valise with a vintage Copacabana Palace hotel label. A shoebox punched with breathing holes dangled from his left hand. Squawking emanated from it, and a beady eye peered out.

"Shh, Zazza," he whispered tipping his hat to a flight attendant.

He wanted to kiss American soil, but there was no way to reach it. He walked through an accordion-like loading bridge toward the arrival gate. In his jet-lagged state, it felt like he was passing through a time tunnel.

As a brash New York entrepreneur, he'd left the Big Apple in 1941 to seek fortune in Brazil. And what fortunes he'd made and lost! Now he was returning to America nearly forty years later, hoping to make his comeback. It was not a propitious time. The America he had left had suffered the Great Depression and was clawing back to fight the Second World War. The America to which he was returning had been defeated in Vietnam, stalled by the oil embargo, held hostage by Ayatollah Khomeini in Iran, and was sinking into a malaise of unemployment.

He gripped his bag and strode into the terminal. The date on the arrivals and departures board was December 9, 1980. He shivered in his tropical suit. Wasn't Miami supposed to be hot? He followed the heels of younger travelers sprinting to arrive first at Passport Control. He straightened his shoulders and strode into the line for U.S. citizens.

The officer fingered the water-stained passport signed by Secretary of State Cordell Hull in 1940 and stamped with the florid seals of South American republics. The officer thumbed back to the ID photo. It depicted a man in his late twenties with jet black hair, parted in the middle; unlined forehead; large, slightly protruding eyes; a prominent, Roman nose; thin, pencil moustache; full lips and square, dimpled chin. He glanced at the man standing before him: wispy hairs on a shiny pate; forehead gouged like a tiled wall missing the grout; surprisingly youthful blue eyes sunken in folds of darkened skin; veined, drooping nose; crooked white moustache, and chin sagging onto the flowered necktie.

"Aren't you going to welcome me back?" Benjamin asked.

"Welcome back -- your passport is expired."

"I'm an American, you can't send me back!"

A guard escorted Benjamin to a windowless room crowded with foreigners speaking all at once. Children huddled on parents' laps. Fathers paced the confined space. Two desperate-faced men emerged from the interview cubicle and were transferred to a holding facility pending deportation. Benjamin set the shoebox down on his lap. An iridescent eye stared from a porthole. The room reeked of tobacco and foreign lands.

A little girl with red ribbons in her braids pointed, "Birdie."

"Shh." Benjamin raised a forefinger to his lips. "It's a secret."

She giggled. Her mother gave him a hostile look and pulled her daughter onto her lap.

An hour later, Benjamin was summoned to the interview room.

"There's been a mistake," he said. "I was born in Brooklyn. I'm as American as apple pie. In fact, I named the Big Apple."

The officer gave him a skeptical look.

"You never heard of the bankrupt millionaires selling apples on the street corners of New York in the Depression?" Benjamin leaned on the metal desk. "I distributed the apples. They called me the Big Apple."

The officer rolled his eyes. "How old are you, Mr. Apple?"

"That's East... Sixty-eight."

"It says here you were born in 1908. That would put you at seventy-two."

"Well, a few years."

"Why are you coming back now?"

Benjamin twisted his wedding ring. "I lost my wife last year."

"I'm sorry to hear that. Where are you going?"

"To visit my brother, Louie East, the Brooklyn Dodger."

"The Dodgers moved to LA in 1958."

"Well, Louie was loyal. He stayed in Brooklyn."

"Is that where you're going?"

"It's my first stop. I've got to publish my book and then take my show on the road." His English was tinged with a Portuguese accent.

"I see." The officer raised his hand. "What's in your bag?"

Benjamin opened the valise, which was tooled in Brazilian leather. He'd winnowed down his worldly goods to a dog-eared manuscript entitled *Pearls*, a few shirts, a wide-lapel suit, striped socks, a faded necktie with coffee bean pattern, and a sepia toned photograph of his wife sunbathing on a beach before the Copacabana Palace Hotel. An alligator skin pouch containing Brazilian gemstones of dazzling colors and varying qualities. A brilliant aquamarine set in an Ouro Preto gold wedding band. A packet of letters on Rio Jockey Club stationery, dated 1942-1958. A box of Novoforma fever medicine and malaria pills. An envelope stuffed with approximately $3,200 in greenbacks and florid cruzeiros. An identification card: Benjamin East, black hair, blue eyes, six foot, one-hundred-eighty-six pounds. Address: Rua dos Passarinhos #31, Rio de Janeiro, Brasil. And a small bottle of Brazilian cologne, labeled *Saudade*, which perfumed the rest of the contents with shades of lavender, citrus, and rum.

The agent checked Benjamin's Custom's Declaration. The gemstones valuation raised an eyebrow.

"Here's the appraisal." Benjamin showed the receipt from H. Stern jewelers valuing the semiprecious gems at $628. The carbon copy's date (1960) was smudged. (The '6' could be an '8.') Benjamin's palms sweated. "They have sentimental value."

"No duty owed, sir," the agent said, to Benjamin's relief. "What's the book about?"

"My life."

The officer broke into a smile at the geezer in the outdated suit and outlandish necktie. He was about to let

Benjamin go, when he heard a squawk. It didn't take him long to discover the shoebox. He frowned. "It's illegal to bring poultry into the United States."

"Zazza's a pet parrot, not a chicken," Benjamin said. "My wife trained her to sing '*Cidade Maravilhosa*'; do want to hear?"

How to explain his love-hate relationship with Zazza without sounding ridiculous? One day, his wife Gisela had found a baby parrot that had fallen out of the nest, on the verge of starvation. She had splinted its broken wing with an ice-cream stick, fed it with an eyedropper, and nurtured it with motherly care. It grew to be a stunted six-inch-tall parrot with nine-inch-long feathers of green, yellow, and orange, streaked like an Amazon sunset. She'd named it Zazza after a telenovela star. They'd chattered in a private language. Benjamin had been grateful she had found a soul companion. But whenever he tried to kiss Gisela, Zazza flew into a rage and tried to peck out his eyes.

Years passed with the squabbling ménage a trois living under one roof. As his ventures failed, Benjamin grew bitter and grumpy. He wanted to give up on himself, but Gisela never gave up on him. Zazza sensed her rival's weakness and dive-bombed when he entered the door. He cursed and flung his crumpled hat at the demon bird. In this absurd soap opera they all played tragicomic roles.

Until one day, he returned and found Zazza screaming bloody murder.

The agent grabbed the box, Benjamin pulled back, and the top flipped off. The agent reached for the trembling creature inside. A green missile shot out and circled over their heads, screaming. Zazza bashed against the wall and dropped to the floor. A feather floated lazily behind. Benjamin sank to his knees and gently lifted Zazza's body. It felt heavy. Her head fell on a limp neck. She had a glassy-eyed stare.

The officer looked on silently with a guilty expression. "I'm sorry, sir."

Benjamin cupped the lifeless creature. Grief pierced his flowered necktie and stabbed his stoic heart. Pain shot through his left arm followed by a wave of nausea. He was holding Gisela in his arms, sorrow pulling him down to the grave. He couldn't bear to lose Zazza, the last living connection.

"Here, sir." The agent offered a handkerchief.

Benjamin carried Zazza across the room to where a file cabinet shielded them from view. He cupped her in his palms and stroked her downy feathers. Whispering in Portuguese, he dabbed the blood off her orange beak. Her gossamer feathers trembled - or were his hands shaking? He drew her beak to his lips and breathed warm air into her. She blinked, revolved her eye, and glared.

"Zazza, you came back!"

She lunged at him and sank her beak into his nose. A jolt of pain jumpstarted his heart, blood surged through his arteries and his reptilian brain nearly strangled her for scaring him half to death. He examined her for injuries, but aside from a bloody beak, she seemed to have survived the ordeal. And this gave him hope.

"A tough little bird." The agent smiled and reached out. "It's time, sir."

"Where are you taking her?"

"Quarantine."

Benjamin pictured tubercular immigrants from the ghettos of Europe, separated from their healthy kin and quarantined at Ellis Island. His mother's great uncle Simon died in the TB ward, within sight of the Statue of Liberty.

"That's a death sentence!"

"Not necessarily. If the bird is disease-free, we return it to the owner. Of course, you pay for health inspections, boarding, and shipping costs. It ain't cheap."

"And if they're infected, do you treat them?"

"We put them to sleep." He tapped his foot. "What do you want to do, Mr. East?"

"I have no choice." Benjamin filled out the paperwork, paid a $75 deposit, and wrote down his brother's address in Brooklyn.

The officer examined the bills under an ultraviolet light and slipped the paperwork into a drawer. "Wait here while I get a container." He returned with a wire cage that would fit a small rodent. "Sorry, it's all we got." He snapped on rubber gloves.

Benjamin nuzzled Zazza. "Keep a stiff upper beak." His lip quivered. Gently, he brushed his nose against her forehead. "I'll wait for you, I promise."

"Enough lovey-dovey." The agent took the bird out of Benjamin's hands. Zazza clawed and bit as she was moved into the cage. She stared out, forlorn.

"Trust Uncle Sam to take good care of your pet." With an ironic smile, the agent discarded the gloves.

"Yeah, like the hostages in Iran." Benjamin had read the headlines in *O Globo* and watched angry Revolutionary Guards shouting "Down with America, the Great Satan!"

Benjamin spotted a single orange flight feather that had fallen to the linoleum floor. He picked up and put it in his breast pocket, where it trembled against his pounding heart.

He loved America the brave defender of freedom, not the cowardly country that took a parrot hostage. He was spoiling for a fight, but not with this little Napoleon.

"When will I get her back?"

"Six to eight weeks. You'll be notified by mail."

A half hour later, Benjamin was given back his passport, stamped 'Temporary Visa.'

"You have ninety days to renew it or face deportation," the agent said with a frown, and then the corners of his lips turned up. "Oh, I almost forgot to say 'Welcome home!'"

It took Benjamin enormous discipline not to punch the bastard's schnozzle. The valise seemed to weigh a ton, but for some stupid reason he couldn't bring himself to throw away the shoebox, so it dangled from his finger as he made his way out of the labyrinth into the reception area. Families embraced relatives, chauffeurs held signs with patrons' names. He had no expectation of being greeted, but still it hurt to walk past tots hugging grandparents, feeling lonesome and invisible. He had no children, no nieces or nephews; he and Louie were the last of the Easts.

He sought sanctuary in a bathroom stall to sit in silence slowly calming down. He splashed water on his face and stared at the haggard mug in the mirror. He ran a wet comb through his wispy hair and used the airline's complimentary shoeshine pad to buff his shoes to a spiffy shine. There was nothing like Shinola to give Benny the Dreamer a little pizzazz. Now he was ready to meet the world. He strode out with a lightness to his step, leaving the shoebox forgotten on the floor, where a janitor would sweep it into the dustbin.

Freedom! He inhaled the recycled air, ran his fingers across glass showcases chock full of electronic gadgetry made in Japan, maneuvered between reunited families chattering in tongues, sped up to the pace of the piped-in Muzak. He felt no culture shock. It was more like a bath of spring water after the sweltering climate of Rio. Why hadn't he come back with Gisela thirty years ago? It didn't matter. He had come back now. As he strode through the crowds and cigarette smoke, he trailed behind him the crisp scent of *Saudade*, a memory of Brazil.

Benjamin found the Greyhound ticket booth at the end of a row of rent-a-car agencies. He leafed through the brochures. There were two deals: For $96 he could get a one-way ticket to New York. Or, for $202, he could buy a *See America Pass* with unlimited travel across the States.

"Any time limit?" he asked the ticket girl peering at him through pink designer specs. Was everyone rich in this country?

"Ninety days, unlimited stops from coast to coast," she tapped her acrylic nails.

"I'll take the *See America Pass*."

He pushed through the glass doors and waited for the connector bus to Miami. There he'd catch the express to Washington, D.C., where he'd stop and get his passport renewed. Then onward to New York to surprise his brother Louie and visit his old stomping grounds. Then, Benjamin East dreamed of California.

The rain had stopped. The sun had risen. Anything was possible here -- still the land of opportunity. A siren wailed in the miasma. A grizzled man wearing a 'POW-MIA' watch cap held out a tin cup. Selling apples gave a man dignity, but times had changed. A penny missed the cup and landed on the pavement. Benjamin stooped down to pick it up and kissed American soil.

CHAPTER 2

The North Star guided the Greyhound from the kudzu of the Deep South to the dogwoods of Virginia, and vanished in the fog as the bus crossed the Potomac River to Washington, D.C.

Benjamin had traveled a thousand miles in twenty-four hours. He'd hobnobbed with a few friendly folks but mostly rode alone. He was alternately amazed and appalled by the vast changes – interstate freeways, shopping malls, and suburban developments bulldozed into the landscape. He couldn't fathom how the richest country in the world had turned its back on the poor. Was America becoming like Brazil?

He toted his valise to the depot in the bowels of Union Station. The ornate clock showed half-past 3 a.m. A janitor swept the floor, which was littered with soda cans, crushed cigarette butts, and yesterday's papers. Benjamin eased his weary bones onto a hard bench, propped up his aching feet, and pulled his hat over his eyes. He'd rest up 'til the passport bureau opened. He fell into a fitful sleep tormented by dreams.

A young woman pushed through the doors and gazed frantically around the depot. She wore sunglasses, a Matisse scarf, a navy blue overcoat, and green suede boots. Her trembling fingers clutched a suitcase with a 'Virginia is for Lovers' sticker. The luggage tags identified her as Amy McCaffrey, and she was running to catch a bus that had left the station five years before. 'I ain't goin' to miss it now.'

She dashed toward the gate, scarf flying behind her.

A bag lady huddled in her path. A Marine dozed on his duffel bag. The janitor sloshed soapy water across the floor. Amy slipped and went flying. She landed on her backside. Her suitcase burst open, flinging a typhoon of lingerie and drawings.

Benjamin awoke with a start. He heard the young woman crying. He eyed her skeptically – one of the new people from nowhere, going nowhere. He tried to ignore her, but everyone seemed to ignore her. She looked like a woman who'd been ignored a good part of her life. Something tugged at his heart. "May I offer you assistance?"

"You really want to help, Mister?" She picked herself off the floor. "Then leave me alone!"

She turned away, clutching her stomach. Her cheeks whitened as she gasped for breath. Pale wrists protruded from her coat sleeves, the skin bruised. Her hands were long and thin, white tendons stretched like violin strings over the bones. Her high-strung hands contradicted the thin plainness of her nose, her pale lips, and flat cheekbones. But red eyes, huge as stop signs, halted him. She was of average height but seemed unaveragely besieged by pain. She bore down on the suitcase, pushing against the chaos inside. With a groan, it shut.

"Sorry, I didn't mean to bark at you." She had a faint Southern accent, and smelled of soap and baby powder. "I just missed my bus."

"You hardly broke the skin." His wrinkled face broke into a smile.

The crumpled hat, old-fashioned suit, and flowered necktie trumpeted Broadway musicals from the 1930s. The vintage New York World's Fair decal on his suitcase emboldened the runaway to reach out.

"Take me to New York!"

What? Is she crazy? Benjamin recoiled in shock. "I've got government business to attend to this morning, but after that..."

"I can't wait," she said. "Ray'll plaster me!"

The outside door opened and she turned, her face exposed to harsh light. Her skin adhered like wet plaster to her bones; the only color was in the creases between her nostrils and her cheeks, a raw pink. Who Ray was, and why anyone would want to plaster her, teased Benjamin's mind as a wizened newspaper vendor dragged his bundle through the door. She muttered to herself, "There's another bus. I've got to go."

She dragged her white deal suitcase toward the ticket line and charged the counter. Her overcoat flew open, revealing long legs in peg-bottomed corduroys, a high waist, and a nasty scratch on her throat.

Benjamin watched as she pushed to the front of the line and was shoved back. She veered toward the departure ramp but was prevented from boarding. She wheeled round and round like a caged bird -- and stopped short.

A man ran toward her as a flock of Japanese tourists obliterated them. Benjamin's eye caught on a blue pastel crayon crushed on the terrazzo. Beyond it lay pastels of emerald and vermilion, the kind artists use; a rainbow of colors had fallen from her bag. Benjamin shook himself from his lethargy, gathered up the pastels, and rushed toward the sound of rising voices.

"Don't touch me!"

"Hush, wife."

"I'm not your chattel." She twisted off her wedding ring and flung it at him. "Give it back to your mama."

"Now Amy," the man drawled. "You're just upset."

"Upset? Yeah, I dreamed up the whole thing."

"When you get finished making a fool of yourself, I'll be waiting in the pickup." He stormed off.

Amy waited until the glass door shut. The silence opened up a terrible shame and hollowness. She stood trembling by the ramp, pale and humiliated in the midst of the dispersing crowd.

Benjamin waited and then brought her the pastels. The colors had come off on his hands.

"Are these yours?" he asked, holding them up.

She looked up, dislocated, and then focused on the pastels. The soft shades seemed to soothe her. She sniffed and smiled, wiping her nose and leaving a streak of ochre.

"Thanks --"

Benjamin turned away, but she caught his sleeve.

"Will you pretend you're with me? If Ray sees me with an older man, he'll know I'm not coming back; he'll go home."

'Are you crazy? I can't get involved,' Benjamin thought, drawing back. But already he was involved. He'd asked if he could help.

Her eyes flared like sunspots. She looked at him straight on. "Last night my husband raped me."

The words slapped him in the face. Either she was lying, or what? Only desperation could make her confess such a thing to a stranger.

"Will you take me to New York now?" she pleaded.

Before he could reply, she ran outside and flagged down a taxi. Benjamin picked up his valise and followed.

"How much to New York?" she asked the driver.

"New York Avenue?"

"No, the Big Apple," Benjamin interceded, puffing out his chest.

The cabby pushed back his yellow cap. He appeared to gape at the weird chick, high on drugs or something, and the geezer in the mothballed suit. "Look, you don't have that kind of money."

"Will two hundred do?" Benjamin dug into his worn leather wallet, a gift from Gisela. The fare was as much as the *See America* ticket, but what could he do? He peeled greenbacks from the billfold. "I'll pay half now."

"Get in."

She started to thank him, but a shout drowned out her words.

She turned and saw Ray running toward them. She grasped Benjamin for support. The dead weight on his shoulders was at least a hundred pounds. Had she fainted? Groaning, he opened the car door. She clutched his necktie and swung onto the back seat. He wanted to walk away from the cab and just keep walking, but something stopped him. Defiance? The beauty and hopelessness made him laugh the old Brazilian Carnival laughter. His stiff knees cracked like dry twigs as he threw in his valise and piled into the cab.

As they pulled away, Amy looked back through the rear window. Ray seemed frozen in motion. Furious and impotent, his motorcycle boots planted on a manhole cover, he raised his middle finger. Then steam rising from subterranean pipes blotted him out.

CHAPTER 3

T he Washington Monument, an obelisk of Vermont marble, is visible from virtually any point in the capital, not for any mystical reason but because federal law prohibits buildings in the District of Columbia from exceeding its 555 foot height. It gives Washington, along with its circles, its broad avenues, its esplanades, a pivotal feeling; as if the world turned around its center. It draws people to the values of freedom, individuality, and democracy embodied by the monument to the Father of Our Country, and communicates by its simplicity, its upward striving.

"What a prick!" Amy cursed the white phallus framed in the rear window.

"Pardon?" Benjamin leaned over the front seat.

"Nothing!"

Benjamin's cologne clashed with the chemical odor emanating from the cab's air freshener. Amy cranked down the window and breathed in the wind. If it were only so easy to let go of the past and not look back. Being who she was, she looked back anyway. Concrete buildings. Trees losing their leaves. Ray was gone. Like her past -- erased; it had never happened. She swiped her hair behind her ears and peered ahead with an alertness that made her look younger than twenty-five, though her skin was drawn and the circles around her eyes made her look washed out -- thirty.

'Where am I going?' Her eyes watered; not tears. It was the wind, the future. She sucked oxygen into her lungs and felt it cleansing her veins, soothing the bruises on her ribs and thighs. New York Avenue was written on the green and white signs they passed on every corner. She looked down the corridor of trees and saw a point where the screwed-up lines of her life would meet at the end of the road and she would come out the other side, a new woman.

An awkward silence enveloped the cab as it whistled past once-elegant townhouses, now burned out tenements. They reached the outskirts of Washington, white suburbs ringing the capital, in reverse of Rio, where the rich lived in the city and the poor were relegated to live without electricity or water in the favelas. Benjamin straightened his tie and looked out the window at the dense green woods pressing up against the highway. He thought of the road up to Petropolis, where Gisela's father had a villa not far from the summer palace of the last emperor of Brazil, and they promenaded through the town in the cool nights and kissed to the batucada of drums. That was not so many years ago. It seemed so close, tangible, not like this road drawn like a ruler through the trees, unreal.

What was he doing in a taxi with a runaway housewife? She huddled in silence in the backseat, tears streaming down her cheeks. Benjamin remembered an Indian maiden he'd once seen crying aboard a tramp steamer on the Rio Negro, sold to prostitution in Belem. He no more knew how to comfort Amy than talk to the natives of the Amazon.

"Mind if I turn on the radio?" the driver asked near Baltimore.

"No, go ahead," Benjamin said, glad to break the silence.

The driver wheeled through the airwaves. He settled on a hard rock station with a disk jockey on amphetamine spinning the discs. The DJ cut away to a traffic copter hovering over a five-mile backup then segued back to the studio for a live interview with a dietitian.

Benjamin cringed. America was suffering from disjunctivitis! Nothing connected. Everything was jammed together. No wonder men were beating up women, wives running away. He wanted to turn to the fugitive in the backseat and say something helpful, but he didn't know the first thing about this new America.

Where had she come from? He shifted in his seat. Ever since he'd stepped off the plane from Brazil, he couldn't get it out of his mind: they've put a man on the moon, they've got enough bombs to kill everyone in the world three times, and here they are, night and day, crowding the highways. What do you do in this country if you've lost your home, your job, your family?

"If you don't mind me asking," he said, leaning over the seatback. "Where do you come from?"

"Virginia."

She'd been born in Harrisonburg, in the Shenandoah Valley, but she'd lived most of her married life in a tract development near Manassas that her husband helped build after coming back from Vietnam. The monumental emptiness defied even the developer's rendition of the Southern plantation manse Ray had picked out of a model home book and built her: a ranch-style Tara with faux pillars. She had lived there for three years, yet she could not remember if the shag carpet had started out blue or beige. It had turned grey, like everything else in her life.

"Do you like Virginia ham?" he asked, knowing little else about the state.

"No, I hate it!"

She saw, reflected in the window, mascara streaked down her cheeks, and a shiver of embarrassment ran through her. She wrestled her leatherette billfold out of her purse and unsnapped the clasp and the greasy scent of pastel crayons rose up in the cab. She pulled out a soiled tissue and blew her nose.

Benjamin wondered if she knew any goose calls.

"Looks like you'll be staying away for a while." He cast a sidelong glance at her stuffed suitcase.

"Forever."

The younger you are, the longer you think you're going to do something. At his age, he didn't want to do anything forever, just today.

"What are you going to do in New York?" he said, offhand.

"I'll show you." She rifled her purse. Her fingers ran over credit cards punched with the raised letters, "Mrs. Ray McCaffrey," claim checks from the dry cleaners for Ray's purple tux jacket and her formal for the Veterans Day Ball at the VFW, a fragile slip of paper with a blue mimeographed message she'd pulled out of a Chinese fortune cookie, "Your wish is within reach." She felt the plastic picture folder, split at the seams and Scotch-taped together, containing her high school graduation portrait, posed in a mortar board supplied by the photographer, her face set in a look of utter vacuity that was supposed to represent a Southern belle, her eyebrows plucked, her tawny red curls ironed flat and pasted across her forehead, from which the acne had been airbrushed, leaving only the green irises deepened by flicks of black eyeliner. She skipped over her parents' 25th anniversary photo and paused momentarily at her wedding portrait: an Instamatic snapshot of Ray in a red bandana, black leather jacket, faded jeans tucked into motorcycle boots, hooking his arm around a pale flower child in front of the E-Z

Motel in Elizabeth City, North Carolina, where they'd eloped. She dug deeper in the detritus of her purse, stabbing her fingertips on hairpins and colored pencils, until she found what she was looking for.

"Here--"

She pulled out a folded-up newspaper clipping from the *Harrisonburg Daily News Record*, "Local girl wins New York art scholarship." It showed an awkward eighteen-year-old hiding her eyes from the camera. She stood next to a painting of a school bus surrounded by protestors. Desegregation battles persisted into the mid-seventies in rural Virginia. The newspaper ink was so smudged you could hardly make out the image. But Amy knew by heart the faces of her classmates staring through the windows of the bus she'd ridden from her father's farm to school in town. Angry protestors marched with placards, "Down with Busing." In the rear window, a white girl and a black boy stared out, their faces fragmented into cubistic shapes. The caption quoted the scholastic prize committee:

"This sensitive painting shows the young artist from the rural South grappling with racism in a naïve style combining pictorial elements of Grandma Moses and Peter Max." And other bullshit, but she wasn't complaining. The scholarship was to Cooper Union Institute in New York.

"That's where I'm going." She handed the yellowed newspaper clip to Benjamin.

"But this was dated several years ago."

"You don't think they'll honor it? I've got the letter in here." She pulled her suitcase onto her knees and started to open it.

"I believe you," he said. "But why did you wait so long?"

She remembered the afternoon she got the letter. Ray had picked her up on his motorcycle and they roared up the side of Massanutan Mountain into the pines. He didn't say a word. She had never seen him act this way before, but it was clear as the newly cut hairs on the back of his head he knew and was afraid of her going away to New York City. Then he parked the bike against a barbed wire fence and lifted her off the seat, and when she started to tell him, he stopped her lips with kisses, his mustache pressing into her nostrils, his hands gripping her wrists. They went down in the dogwood leaves, which crunched like cereal and sent motes of dust into the shafts of sunlight streaming through the branches. He proposed to her afterwards. She lay on her back in the prickly leaves with her bare thighs cooling in the pine breeze, and he promised her he'd take her to Alaska. He'd work on the pipeline and she'd draw Eskimos and icebergs, not sterile nudes in a dusty studio.

When she told him she didn't know, he got mad and cut himself pulling the bike off the fence, and as they took the curves down the mountain, swinging toward the smoke rising from the Shenandoah, they seemed to fall together into the turns, like a pendulum or like fate, and she knew she would keep the letter hidden in the bottom of her drawer.

"I married Ray instead," she said. "We were getting ready to go to Alaska when he got Greetings from Uncle Sam. When he came back from Nam, he had tracks in his arms. You know how that goes."

"No, I don't."

"Smack."

"He hit you?"

"That too. But to get off heroin, he got hooked on Jesus."

"Why didn't you both go to New York?"

"Ray didn't want to."

Benjamin nodded, one mystery solved. Now, the bigger and messier question.

"Do you want to talk about what happened?"

"Oh, that! I just said it to get your attention," she laughed breezily, covering her wrists. "Where are you coming from -- Brazil?"

"How did you guess Brazil?"

"The sticker on your suitcase. Were you down there on vacation?"

"Sort of. I left the frozen canyons of Manhattan in February of '41, and took a Pan-Am Flying Boat down to Carnival in Rio. I stayed thirty-nine years."

"Why Brazil?"

"Imagine a country as big as America without a road through its center. Then picture a rainforest as vast as Europe, rich in resources. Brazil was the last frontier."

That was his pat answer. But when he used to lie on his cot at night and stare up at the thatch roof dripping in the rain and feel the hut shake and hear, across the palms, the sea pounding on the beach, he didn't know why he had come to that strange shore. It was a mystery -- like Gisela. Brazil had attracted him with its physical immensity, which he took for promise, and it seduced him with its exotic beauty, which he believed was just blossoming. It grabbed him and lifted him to heights and tossed him down like a coconut.

"Why'd you come back?" she said.

Benjamin twisted the ring on his finger. He had answers for that too. The Big Apple had made its comeback, and he wanted to cut off a slice. And there were practical reasons; to see his brother and sell his book. But when, in Rio, he had stared into the sea shimmering with unutterable beauty and thought of returning to the canyons of New York, he pictured the salmon that is born in mountain streams and migrates to the wide blue sea, then swims back upstream, leaping up waterfalls -- to spawn the next generation.

"To see America."

CHAPTER 4

"Benny!" Lou's voice rattled from the other side of the eye-slit. Benjamin's chin trembled. He heard three locks spring open and a pole squeak; then the door jerked wide and there was old iron arms standing in his undershorts: six feet of knees and white hair shining like ticker tape, beaming like the day he'd hit his first home run.

"Louie, lemme look at ya!"

A man three inches taller and twenty pounds lighter than Benjamin stared back from the doorway. For Benjamin, it was like seeing himself reflected in a convex mirror: round pate made oval; the face was elongated, features hanging like skin separated from bones. Lou's shoulders were broader, pulled down by his apelike arms. His hands dwarfed Benjamin's. His chest was sunken, but his belly was bigger than Benjamin's, as if the brothers' flesh had been molded by the same sculptor holding one figure upside down. Who was right side up? That was the question! The greatest difference was in the eyes: Benjamin's were light blue, protruding like bay windows; Louie's were small and brown, set under eave-like brows. "You look terrific," Benjamin lied, shocked by what age had done to his brother, blind to its effects on himself. He grabbed Lou's head and crushed him to his chest. "Hey Hitter!" He sputtered, squeezing away the rivalry and feeling the body cleave to his body, overhang to underhang, making him feel almost whole. "Ole Fly Ball. Brother, did I miss you!"

They careened blindly against the umbrella stand, their sinews twining like banyan roots. Benjamin smelled his father's onion breath, felt his mother's arthritic hands in Louie's embrace. He remembered, as if watching a silent movie, the morning Pop had come back from the sanatorium in New Jersey, straw boater cocked on his pink head, a dozen red roses for their mother, and announced he was cured of pleurisy. It was 1927, the height of the stock market boom, the green grocery was prospering, and Pop was full of plans to start a chain of markets. He walked in the door, gave each boy a punch on the chin, and swept Lily up in his arms. The family danced in a circle on the wood floor of the grocery. A year later Pop was dead and Benjamin had left home.

"Now don't you run off again!" Louie cried, kissing his cheeks.

"Who said I'm running off?"

"You did, in your letter. You're stopping by on the way to California."

"We'll talk about that later. I want you to meet somebody."

Louie looked over his brother's shoulder and nearly dropped his false teeth. A pale straggly redhead sporting hunter green boots was standing beyond the door. Her cheeks were gaunt, her hair like a sunset hurricane. A blue woolen overcoat trailed from her shoulders.

As he looked at her with her white suitcase braced against her knee, her reddened eyes drove his stare to the floor.

"Amy, this is my brother Louie, a Brooklyn Dodger," he said. "Lou, Amy is an art student. She's on her way to Cooper Union."

"Charmed," Lou said, taking her hand. It was cold as a refrigerated whitefish. Her cuticles were bitten red. "Ben, can I speak to you a minute alone?"

"Sure." Lou closed the door. Benjamin smiled slyly and sniffed a sharp, sickening odor. He coughed. Camels? Tampas? The air in the apartment was blue as a pool hall, but the smell was fetid and sterile -- a hospital odor. He looked suspiciously around the living room at the piles of funnies and used dishes, packs of playing cards and curled, half-burned matches. His eyes fell on a grey breathing mask connected to a plastic tube. "Lou, what's that thing -- an oxygen tank?"

"Nothing," Lou scoffed, angry at Ben for not telling him when he was coming so he could have hidden the breathing apparatus. "It's just a vacuum pump for the quacks to suck out my money." Lou coughed, waving Benjamin off. All this talk was plugging his lungs with phlegm, but he still had to explain. "See, you hook it up to your pockets and it sucks your money right out."

"Why didn't you tell me you were sick? I never would have brought her."

Lou could barely breathe, but he was not about to have Ben's homecoming ruined by his emphysema. And the broad was a bonus.

"Ben, we haven't missed each other for all these years to start by talking crap," he coughed, turning red, then blue. "This lung thing's under control. Now tell me," he asked, licking his chops. "Where did you meet her?"

"In the combat zone of the Washington bus station. She's in trouble. It's a long story, but she got me to hijack a taxi to New York."

Louie slapped his thigh. "Ben, you brought a dame ... in a taxi ... from Washington!" Louie's laughter triggered a cough that rattled deep inside his chest and rose like leaves wadding a drain spout.

"Lou?" Benjamin shouted, reaching for the oxygen mask.

"Nothing, nothing," hacked the barefoot man. "Be over ... just a ... minute." He straightened, wiped his eyes. "Ben, of course I can put her up. Fix her some dinner!

I've got some corned beef and cabbage, a little spaghetti, half a Chinese dinner. If she's not feeling so hot, I can make her some chicken soup," he whispered, wagging his head. "Jesus, you haven't changed since your Big Apple days. Still the humanitarian. You know you're famous? Not you, the Big Apple. If you had copyrighted that name you could sue for a million dollars!"

Benjamin smiled weakly, shaking his head.

Louie turned aside, burdened by something he'd been holding in since he'd received Benjamin's last letter.

"Ben, I'm sorry to hear what happened to your wife." He groped for words, feeling terrible about a foreign sister-in-law he'd never met. "I know she must have been a wonderful gal to keep you down there all these years. But now," he hesitated. "You're back. We're together. We'll visit Mama and Pop."

"Mama and Pop?"

"Pop's yarzheit is coming up. Aren't you going to pay your respects at the cemetery?"

"I've had enough death this year, Lou. Can't we postpone it? He's been dead for fifty years."

"You're the oldest son, Ben. And you've never seen Mama's grave."

"All right, Lou, I'll go if it will make you happy."

"And then we'll get busy. I've got some plans for you, Mr. Big Apple! We'll get you back into the fruit business."

"Lou, I appreciate it, but let's talk about plans later. Okay Slugger?" He slapped his brother on the shoulder. "We won't just go back to the old times. We'll move forward. I'll show you my latest project -- a book!"

"A book?"

"Yeah, didn't I write you about it? I thought I included a chapter in the letter."

"Oh that, I thought it was a joke."

"Very funny. It's going to be a bestseller and buy us a beach house in California." He pulled out his *See America* ticket. "Look Lou, for $200 we can cross the country."

"Now you've got me going, too. When the Dodgers abandoned Brooklyn, I vowed I'd never set foot in Los Angeles!"

"How about San Francisco?"

"I'm not game." Louie lit a cigarette. His lungs sucked up the calming smoke and he grimaced. "Look Ben, you've been travelling for a week. Your head's still up in the clouds. We'll talk about this when your feet are back on the ground. Now, how about some dinner? That dame must be tired of waiting."

"Oh my God, I forgot all about her. You don't mind?"

"Mind? It's better than talking to a wild man," Lou smiled, then disappeared, coughing, in a cloud of smoke.

Benjamin winced and opened the door. The hallway was empty.

Maybe she'd gone down to wait in the lobby. In the elevator, he leaned against the graffiti and grieved at the nightmare of Lou coughing and lighting up: Lou, who had stolen bases, now chained to an oxygen tank. He shivered and rubbed his temples. Lou was scared. Ben could smell it in the rancid air in the apartment: the odor of decaying potato peels, yellowed T-shirts, and dusty mementos of his days as a star. It was good he'd come home; Lou needed him. A few days together and he'd knock some life into the old flesh and bones, put him back in the pink of health.

The elevator hit the ground floor and Benjamin ran out. The entryway was also empty. A draft blew through the open door.

To hell with her! Better to be with his own flesh and blood. But he looked outside and saw Amy standing at the curb with her white deal suitcase and her country girl appearance, a woman from nowhere going somewhere. He bolted out the door and waved his hands, pulled by something in Amy he couldn't name, but a quality he knew the East brothers needed tonight.

"Hey, wait! Don't you want to hear about the Brooklyn Dodgers?"

"I'm intruding."

"Where are you going? It's dark--"

"Don't worry about me." She put out her hand. "Thanks. I'll pay you back someday."

"Hey." He squeezed her fingertips. "You're the first young artist who's listened to my story. After you get into Cooper Union and I sell my book, we'll celebrate. Okay?"

"It's a deal." She let go of his hand and climbed into a cab.

"Wait, here's Louie's number." He scrawled it on a scrap of paper.

"Thanks for everything."

"My pleasure." Benjamin watched the cab go around the corner. Then he walked slowly upstairs.

CHAPTER 5

T he following Monday, Benjamin slipped on his grey flannel suit, crept past Louie crumpled asleep on the sofa -- Lou had insisted he take the bed -- lifted his manuscript out of the valise and sneaked out the door in his bare feet. The hall floor was cold on his soles, invigorating. He slipped on his tropical weight socks, buffed his shoes on the threadbare carpet, held them up to the light for inspection, and lit out on the streets dawning with rush-hour traffic.

As a former salesman, he knew he should check out his territory before paying any visits. Selling a book was no different than selling an apple -- you just had to convince the customer it was what he needed. Getting the product to the man on the street was the challenge -- you had to get around the middleman -- and the best way to do that was to go straight to the top.

But first, he wanted to pay his respects to New York.

He told the taxi driver to head to the Empire State Building, and he leaned out the window and counted up thirty-one floors to a barely visible niche, the picture window of his former office, rented for a song when the tallest building in the world was nearly vacant, where he had looked down at the streets and felt he could grasp New York in one hand. Forty-three years fused together in the first red gleam of sun glinting off the panes.

He returned to the corners on Wall Street that his vendors had brightened with fruit in 1930, when the Depression blacked out half the shop windows and the only color was the apples sold by bankrupt businessmen in front of their former stores and offices.

You couldn't pin down the origin of the name, Big Apple, any more than you could explain why the apple vendors became a symbol of the Depression. But he had built up an organization of vendors and had been nicknamed the Big Apple before he ever heard it refer to the City, and so he could claim ownership of a sort to the title. But what would it get him? With the Big Apple and a nickel, he could buy a cup of coffee. No, you needed fifty cents today at Chock Full O' Nuts. The Depression had become the Recession. The unemployed were returning to the streets. The lessons of the past were forgotten. A lone flower lady sold roses on the corner. He waved, unrecognized.

He looped back to the publishing district. His eyes threw a penny in the fountain of the Plaza Hotel, where

F. Scott and Zelda Fitzgerald had taken a bath in the Twenties, when the rich were supposed to be different, when Benjamin had to drop out of school to help his father at the grocery in Brooklyn. He wished for one thing: to see his book, *Pearls*, in the window of Scribner's bookstore. A self-educated man, he had always revered writers as the ultimate salesmen. They took the cheapest substance in the world -- ideas -- and made them into valuable properties.

Benjamin was an eclectic reader. As a young man, he'd discovered travel through Richard Halliburton's *Book of Marvels*. He'd once taken off three days from work to read *Anthony Adverse* straight through. But since he'd gone to Brazil, his reading had tended toward nonfiction: minerals, history of Brazil, business etc. Wendell Wilkie's *One World* had inspired him. He read the Brazilian newspapers *Jornal do Brasil* and *O Globo* religiously. But the only book he'd labored through in Portuguese was Machado de Assis' *Epitaph of a Small Winner*, which he didn't understand, but from which he salvaged a quotation: "It is a wonderful advantage to have been endowed by heaven with the gift of seeing the relationship between things that are apparently unrelated. I had this gift, and even today I am grateful for it from the bottom of my grave." Another favorite quotation was from Mark Twain: "A man who goes around with a prophecy-gun ought never to get discouraged. If he will keep up his heart and fire at everything he sees, he is bound to hit something by and by." Originally, he put these two quotations at the beginning of *Pearls*, but they were too negative, so he removed them from the final copy.

Benjamin had no pretensions about art. But he believed it would be easy to become a best-selling author because his message was addressed to simple people interested in bettering themselves; and if a book could help them in their lives, then it would be worth the investment.

What was unique about *Pearls?* he asked himself, practicing his sales pitch. A man's hard-knocks experience was packed into every chapter. The characters weren't literary, but easy to relate to, like cartoon characters in a comic strip. The plot was not artificial but like life itself; it went off in many directions at once, hit dead ends and headed back again to the goal: to take difficulties and make something lasting. It wasn't art for art's sake - it had a message. And what's more, unlike the how-to books he'd perused in the U.S. consulate library in Rio, you didn't need to buy any equipment, or adopt a religion, or meditate, or jog; you just used your own memories and hopes. The book had everything you needed in it. The whole kitchen sink. "A cornucopia!"

"What, you say something to me?" asked the taxi driver.

"No, let me off here."

He stepped out on Madison Avenue, the heart of the publishing district. He walked past the offices of the major publishers and settled on one.

"What floor is the publisher's office?" he asked the doorman.

"Of which division?"

"The whole army."

Benjamin waved his hand and entered the elevator before the doorman could stop him. He punched the top button and sailed up to the 36th floor.

A receptionist looked up from her compact mirror at the man in the outdated suit who strode out of the elevator extending a hand to his reflection in a floor-to-ceiling mirror. He stopped and looked around like a guilty boy. Finally, he saw her and took off his hat.

"That mirror fools a lot of people." She put away the case and slipped her pointy glasses over her heavily mascaraed eyes. Her makeup made her look bruised. "Are you delivering that? I can sign for it." She reached for the parcel clutched in his hand.

"No, I'd prefer to give it to him myself." Benjamin held onto the manuscript. It was a bit humiliating to be taken for a delivery boy, but humiliation was the name of the salesman's game. It made victory all the sweeter.

"Who's it from?" she asked.

"Ah, special delivery from Brazil."

"Oh, really. I didn't know we had any authors down there."

"You don't, yet."

A red security light flashed on her console. The phone rang and she picked it up and started talking.

Just then, the teak door opened and a thin, owl-eyed man in his thirties stuck his head into the reception room. "Could you get me some fresh coffee?" he asked the secretary, jiggling an empty cup. "I'm on the phone."

The receptionist was busy talking and didn't hear. But Benjamin leapt from his chair and came forward, outstretching his hand to introduce himself. The publisher put the cup in it.

"Cream?" Benjamin asked, displaying the courtly grace of a waiter at the Jockey Club.

"Thanks." The publisher smiled, his features separating into a boyish grin.

Seeing his opportunity to get into the inner office, Benjamin rushed over to the coffee table in the copy room, poured coffee from an urn and, juggling the cup and fixings on the tray of his manuscript, brought it into the office and shut the door behind him.

"Don't give up the movie rights!" the executive was saying. "The book is nothing without a Hollywood sale." He saw Benjamin standing before him. "Set it down there."

Benjamin cleared a landing place, poured in the cream, stirred it twice, clinking the cup with the spoon, ripped open a pink packet and poured saccharine into the brown water. He felt that passive power of servants over their masters.

The publisher smiled, nodding thanks. He slammed down the phone and rolled his eyes. Benjamin winked back and pushed his manuscript forward. A drop of coffee beaded on the title page.

"I know how you feel about Hollywood," Benjamin said. "These writers are getting away with murder. On this property, you can have the movie rights."

"What property?" asked the publisher, wheeling back in his chair.

"It's a South American author. They're getting very big now. I wanted you to have the first chance at it."

"I don't remember--"

"The book transcends continents and decades, bringing together the Amazon --"

The publisher cringed and interrupted: "Do you have an appointment?"

"No, but I thought you'd be interested."

"You don't just barge into people's offices."

"I wanted to show you my ingenuity. If I can make it in here, I can make it to the top of the best-seller list."

"Maybe so. But there are rules. You can send our acquisition editor a letter of inquiry. If she's interested, she'll ask you to submit the first fifty pages and an outline. Then she may wish to see the whole book. Now if you'd be so good as to leave, I have some work to do."

The door opened. Benjamin kept trying to explain, but a guard grabbed his elbow. Benjamin shook him away and shouted, "I'm Benjamin East. Haven't you ever heard of the Big Apple?"

The publisher blushed as the guard pulled him backward. Benjamin broke free, got his manuscript and walked to the elevator, standing straight and tall.

It wasn't the first time in his life he'd been shown the door. Nothing ventured, nothing gained, he told himself, walking down Fifth Avenue. Maybe he'd been a little too forward. But this letter-of-inquiry business could take months. Better to get some names of editors and write them a little note of introduction. One by one, he made the rounds of publishers, getting names and addresses. Exhausted, he caught a cab to Louie's apartment.

The sun was falling. He leaned forward, trying to recapture the landmarks, and told the driver about the apple vendors and the rest, seeing if he believed it.

"Those were the days." The driver pushed back his hat and flashed a crinkled smile. "I remember Mayor LaGuardia reading the comics on the radio during the newspaper strike."

The cab passed the Essex House where he'd kept a penthouse overlooking the park, and blind jazz pianist Art Tatum used to tickle the ivories at the bar and the elegant diners gorged themselves on T-bone steaks, oblivious to the faces of hungry people pressed up against the window. He winced: it was now a chain hotel.

"Where are my limousines, my ladies in mink?" he crooned.

The taxi wheeled around Columbus Circle and Benjamin saluted the statue of the discoverer of the New World, old and abandoned as a bag lady in traffic. They headed up Central Park West. To the right, the trees of Central Park, lit by the sunset, glowed pink as Corcovado at dawn. But to the left, the battlement apartment houses that once marched uptown in a parade of brownstone and brass now looked battered, shabby. In front of the Museum of Natural History, the equestrian statue of Teddy Roosevelt, explorer of the Amazon, discoverer of the River of Doubt, a tributary which Benjamin had also explored, was spray-painted with obscenities. He felt personally attacked and held onto the strap with two hands, watching the streets converge with the setbacks of his life. The misery of Spanish Harlem was painfully familiar, a favela slum ripped from the hilltops of Rio and dumped in the shadow of Morningside Heights.

"What's happened to New York?" he asked in despair.

"Haven't you heard? It's the capital of the Third World."

"Don't put down the Third World. I lived in Brazil and it was beautiful!"

"Then why didn't you stay there?"

The window blurred; Benjamin wiped away tears. "I've seen enough."

He retreated into silence for the remainder of the ride. Opening his billfold to pay the driver, he came across a snapshot of Gisela dancing on the swirling mosaic sidewalk of Copacabana.

The driver wondered what was taking so long; he looked around and saw the man blinking over his open wallet.

"You owe me fourteen dollars. That's a buck discount for entertaining me with that stretcher about the Big Apple," he said with a wink.

"Hard to believe, eh?" Benjamin put away the photo.

"Not at all. You should go on 'What's My Line?' Maybe someone would remember."

The downstairs buzzer was broken. So was the lock to the front door. *Can't the landlord even keep the place in repair? When Louie moved in, it was a middle-class residence. Now it's a slum.* Benjamin's heart labored as the ancient elevator creaked up six floors. Treading down the corridor, past the familiar cracked seashell light shades, the black barricaded doors, the open trash chute, he wondered why he had come back.

"Your first day home and you sneak off to go downtown!" Lou kibitzed, burning hamburgers on the skillet. "You look like you could use a drink."

"Thanks."

"So how did it go?"

"I had some ups and downs," he shrugged. "But I'm learning the ropes."

"By the way, that girl called."

"Did she leave a number?" he asked, brightening.

"No, I thought you had hers."

"Any message?"

"Yeah, she said, 'Tell him I found Cooper Union and I'm looking forward to his publishing party.'"

CHAPTER 6

B enjamin and Louie left the discount flower shop at Washington Cemetery, carrying a memorial wreath for their parents. They drove to the graveyard, where the tombstones were crowded so close that the dead had to stand on their feet. Benjamin thought he saw a woman in a blue overcoat running down a path lined with plastic flowers. Louie was trying to convince him to buy a cemetery plot and compose his own grave inscription. The woman disappeared, like all the other fresh-faced, country-looking women Benjamin had almost hailed since coming to New York. He was surprised at himself for looking for Amy. She was as un-reachable as the business coups of his apple days, his rev-els in Brazil.

Over the weeks, he'd taken his book to half a dozen Madison Avenue publishing houses and been roundly turned away. In the end, only one secretary said she'd give it to an editor to read. Benjamin had exaggerated a little about the plot, leaving out the hero, Sandy, and the mixed metaphors, and saying the book was "the inside story of New York in the Depression, told by the man who named the Big Apple." She shook her head but took his manuscript. Now he was waiting for an answer. Weeks had passed. Louie and his obituaries depressed him. Approaching the burial site, he felt he was being invited back to join the family obelisks that mocked the skyscraping dreams he'd strived for in life.

"Come on, Lou, let's quit talking up this grave business," Benjamin forced a laugh. "We're not moving into this rest home yet. After I publish my book, we'll retire in California and pick grapefruit for breakfast!"

Lou gripped the steering wheel, pretending not to hear the hype about traveling. Ben had been barraging him with it for the last week.

"You can't live forever, Ben. You've got to plan ahead. Stay with the people who love you." Lou meant the dead.

Benjamin turned, gripped the wreath. It filled the car with the nauseating odor of flowers bred to smell like regret, like sorrow. Why couldn't mourners simply pluck wildflowers for the graves, as people did in Brazil?

They reached their parents' plot: two roughly hewn stones lettered with immigrant names, Lily's carved twenty years after Jacob's. Louie's sad, pious manner caused guilty stirrings within Benjamin. He prayed, imagining his mother's hands catching at the wind, the old man's gold buttons shining, Louie's voice echoing in his ear.

"They should plant trees, not tombstones!" Benjamin cried. "Imagine if graveyards were turned into orchards."

Lou approached the grave, took a lily from the wreath, and gave it to Benjamin.

"This is for Gisela," Lou said.

Benjamin looked up, grateful, then leaned down and laid the flower gently on the cold American earth.

"What happened to her, Ben? You can tell me."

Benjamin turned, gnarled with grief. Had Louie given him the lily to stab like a dagger into the wound?

Memories tugged him down. Gisela had held his hand and jumped off roofs with him for thirty years: crystal, uranium, refrigerators, damming the Amazon. She never hesitated to go along with his magnificent plans. Since he had arrived in Rio with a letter of credit to the Banco do Brasil, Brazil's gross national product had multiplied by ten. The new capital, Brasilia, had soared like an airplane from the Altiplano. A Trans-Amazon highway had been bulldozed through the heart of the Amazon.

And Benjamin?

He had made $20,000 in crystal, lost it pursuing uranium deposits in the jungle, and recouped a few thousand in import-export. He borrowed to buy an appliance factory and lost everything in the inflation of the early 1960s. He'd hurtled downward from there, tugging his dreams and his wife behind him, cornering old friends with proposals to invest in semi-precious stones. He haunted the Jockey Club reading room and cadged drinks at the Copacabana Palace bar. Hung-over, he'd tumbled out of bed with malarial nightmares and plunged into the Atlantic to wake himself up.

Still falling, falling.

Unable to stop, he'd dragged sand into the house and taken a shower. Toweling himself off, he felt a little better, and tightened the Windsor knot in his necktie. Admiring the Fifth Avenue label, he remembered the day he'd marched into Macys and bought a dozen white-on-white linen shirts because he liked the shimmery fabric.

Yes, sir! He had made it to the top of New York once, he could make it again in Rio, if he could just get a handhold somewhere, smiling in the corroded mirror and combing back his wisps of hair, rubbing on cologne, whistling through the hallway to tell Gisela everything was coming up roses.

She didn't answer. The curtains blew in the kitchen window.

He leaned forward to close them and looked out and down and gripped the sash. Gisela lay crumpled in her flowered dressing gown on the balcony, a potted geranium she had been watering broken beside her. The doctor said the cause of death was a mixture of alcohol and pills. But her priest said it was suicide and wouldn't let her be buried. Benjamin blamed himself. It was then that he started writing.

"Ben, are you all right?"

Benjamin opened his eyes and looked about him, disoriented.

The first lines of his book came to his lips. "How does a grain of sand turn into a pearl?" he asked.

"What?" barked Louie. "Ben, what's wrong with you? You're talking to yourself! Since you've been home, you've been acting desperate. You've got to face whatever happened. She'd dead! Preaching so-called pearls of wisdom can't bring her back. You'll join her in a better place." He looked upward. "We're lucky. We come from the old days. We're not like these people you meet nowadays. These phony runaways--"

"It's from what I wrote in *Pearls*," Benjamin stammered, unwilling to accept his brother's fatalism. "What does an oyster know about a grain of sand?" he asked, seeing the trashed cemetery as the filth and pain and suffering of their lives. "Does it have to be an expert to fill in the pearly layers? You see, the world is as big as an elephant or small as a grain of sand, depending on you. You can let it stomp you, gore you, swallow you up. Or you can let it slip into your shell and turn into a pearl."

Ben opened his eyes, hoping he'd shown Lou the meaning of *Pearls*, believing for a moment that his brother would accept it. Lou stared at him, his mouth agape.

Encouraged, Benjamin puffed himself up. "Universal message, huh? It's being considered by a famous publisher, and I've got ideas how to syndicate it in newspapers, make a movie. Look, Lou, I know your lungs hurt, but if you'd just read my book, I think you might break out of this cemetery in your mind. When I sell it, we'll get you a bus ticket and cross the country together."

"Why do you want to do that?"

"To see America."

"What does that mean?" Lou demanded. "That's an escape. You're going to head off into the sunset and never come back!"

"What's left for me here?"

"Look, Ben. You're not going to get the money to finance this trip anyway."

"What do you mean?"

"I'm not going to California, and you aren't either," he said. "Ben, I didn't know how to tell you. A secretary called this morning. Your book was rejected."

Benjamin shook his head. "What did she really say?"

"The editor threw a fit! Apparently, you misled her about the contents, and she put herself on the line. A woman deceived. She said the only publisher who'd print it would be a vanity press, and you'd have to fork out several thousand bucks. She insisted you not call her. She's leaving the manuscript with the doorman."

Benjamin stared at the wreaths, which now seemed to memorialize his hopes. "Then I'll go back and publish it in Brazil. All the big books are coming from South America now."

"You're finished!" Louie shouted, followed by a fit of coughing, but that didn't stop him. "And if you go back to that shit-pot, that's where you belong!" With one shoulder, Louie backed Benjamin over a tombstone and pinned him.

"For God's sake Ben, I read your book myself," Lou panted, the exertion beginning to catch up with him. "Pearls, grains of sand. What kind of nonsense is that? You're not a writer. You're a fruit salesman! Everything you've tried since has turned bad. And you dragged Gisela down into it, too. Well, you're not gonna do it to me.

"Now listen, I've got an offer for you. While you've been puttering around publishers, I've been talking to friends. There's a fruit store on Long Island looking for a character to attract business. It's the best thing that's going to come down the pike for the likes of you. And if you take the job, I'll consider moving with you to a retirement condominium, beautiful place I know overlooking the expressway. Take it, Ben!" Louie released him from the tombstone and picked up Benjamin's hat. "They're calling tonight. Will you talk to them?"

Benjamin looked at the graves, littered with trash. Didn't they maintain public cemeteries anymore? He remembered when it was different, when dirty work wasn't considered beneath you. He had hired bankrupt stockbrokers to sell apples on the street corners of New York. They were grateful not to be reduced to begging.

Standing in the snow, they sold frosty apples to the fortunate people who were still working.

Snow Apples, they called them.

He was lucky to have grown up in the fruit markets. He cobbled together apple crates to make his first stand, and built the business from the bottom up. He worked on the principle that you could never make money without having people work for you, and people wouldn't work unless there was some way to profit, no matter how small. He had tried selling oranges and watermelons and grapefruit, but apples were the fruit that caught on. They were red. You could shine them. They tasted sweet. And there was the free advertising: the Garden of Eden brand. Those were the good days, before he made money in real estate and went to Brazil. Perhaps his days could be good again. And maybe Louie was right. Benjamin didn't want to travel alone.

"Okay, I'll talk to them," he said, throwing up his hands.

"That's what I like to hear! That's my old Benny! We'll get the fruit store to put up a Big Apple poster, and you'll wear one of those 'I Love New York' T-shirts, and a red button --" He tottered, overcome by a fit of coughing, and had to be propped up.

It was so easy to submit, Benjamin acquiesced, helping Louie back to the car. "The Wages of Sin Is Death!" thundered a billboard. Benjamin smiled, converted to fatalism. How above it all Louie's railroad apartment seemed now. How comforting the darkness. He sank into the easy chair littered with ashes and breathed in the smoky air, letting his eyes rest on the TV, the electronic confession box that absolved his sins, leaving him simon-pure as a stiff decked out on a bier for the great home-coming voyage.

The phone awakened him with a start.

"Hello?" he muttered, barely audible, tangled in cords. "One second--" he covered the phone. "Lou, it's a wom-an! You didn't tell me I'd have to work for a woman!"

"It's the boss's secretary. Go ahead, like a mensch!"

"Yes, about that position--"

Laughter cascaded in his ear.

"Who is this?"

"Benjamin, you sound so serious."

"Amy!" He covered the receiver, *"Hey Lou, it's the bud-ding artist calling.* How's New York treating you? Do you like Cooper Union?"

"I--"

"Where are you now?"

"At the Museum of Modern Art."

"What are you doing there?"

But she couldn't explain wandering among the paint-ings trying to understand the meaning of *primitive.* Dounier Rousseau's canvas, *The Dream,* had wrapped her in a hypnotic embrace. The overlapping leaves, the hot-house flowers, the paralyzing vegetation that choked the sky, while a flautist played to a naked woman on a divan and lions lurked in the foliage.

"I showed them my letter and they about laughed in my face," she said. "They looked at some sketches I did of Greenwich Village. They told me to go back to Virginia. Paint my family, paint the house. They called me primitive."

"Primitive?" Benjamin said. "In New York! Who do they think built this city, the hoity-toity?" So she had been rejected too. The city had no more respect for the young than the old, the countrywoman or the prodigal. "Hello? I can't hear you."

"I'm crying."

"What?"

"Crying!"

"Don't touch the wires. You might electrocute yourself."

"I don't care."

"That's what Picasso said when he cut off his ear."

"It was Van Gogh!"

"See? You're talking like an artist. What do you need school for?"

"I don't know. How did your homecoming go?"

"My book has gotten unbelievable reactions in New York," Ben said. "I'm being encouraged to publish it outside the traditional framework."

Louie almost fell out of his chair. "Tell her to call back," he pleaded, leaping up and pacing in his carpet slippers. "You're expecting an important call!"

"Huh?" Amy said. "Where are you going?"

"San Francisco."

"Ach, God!" Louie clapped his palm on his forehead.

"I can't hear--"

"San Francisco, the Rio of America! I'm going to cross the U.S.A., sell *Pearls* like I sold apples. First, I have to make final arrangements with one of those avant-garde publishers out there. Then of course I'll have to discuss the movie rights."

"Phony! You'll kill yourself wandering!" Lou shouted.

"What's your brother saying?"

"He's, uh, inviting you to a farewell party he's throwing for me at the Stardust Room."

"I'll throw you out right now!" Infuriated, Lou hurled Benjamin's valise at his feet and began pelting him with shorts and socks.

"Amy, smooth yourself into some silk stockings and meet us for dinner Friday night." Benjamin ducked a shoetree. "The Stardust Room will slink the primitivity right out of you."

He hung up and turned slowly to face his brother.

"Lou, I appreciate your efforts to find me a job, but when they call I'm going to politely tell them no. I'm sorry, but--"

"You sorry old fool!" Lou stomped away and slammed the door.

CHAPTER 7

Amy lay on the Castro Convertible bed at the Delroy Hotel and stared between her bruised elbows at the ceiling, drifting between wakefulness and sleep. She had ordered a shower and was waiting for the clank that signaled they'd turned on the hot water in the bathroom at the end of the hall. The ceiling was plaster. Real plaster. The pocked surface, traversed by cockroaches, pinned her on the bed. After leaving Louie's apartment, she'd taken a room at the Delroy without looking at the furnishings, pulled down the yellowed shades, bolted the door, and fallen into a drowning sleep. Sometime in the dishwater grey dusk, she'd awakened and looked up at the ceiling with shock. It was as if Ray had followed her in and locked the door behind him. She'd had relived that terrible memory every night she'd spent at the Delroy since.

"I don't feel like making love tonight," she'd said.

"You got your thing in?" he bellowed in the dark.

"I forgot."

"We'll see!" He tore open her nightgown, the French negligee he'd brought back from Saigon. He wound the nightie around his wrist and pulled, flipping her on her back. Knocking the wind out of her.

"I'll do it for you."

"No! Gawd!"

Elbows pinning knees, fingers groping flesh, Ray's stucco-hardened hands knew how to handle an uncooperative machine. The compressor bucks and screams, fighting the operator. But the nozzle is built to receive white epoxy and to spit out stucco. The machine wants to function, but it needs a man to show it how.

He twisted her neck ninety degrees and shoved her face into the pillow. The diaphragm slipped out of reach, so like Amy. Not this time. He clawed it out. Amy jackknifed.

"Ms. McCaffrey." Napoleon, the Delroy's night clerk, banged on the door. She stared at the walls, the crack on the ceiling, the neon lights blinking from a movie house. Above the rooftops, she saw the Chrysler Building, cool as ivory, shining in the darkness.

"Hot water!" shouted Napoleon.

"Thanks." Amy propped herself up on her elbow and gazed wanly at the keyhole. She wanted to roll on her back and die, like a cockroach, but she summoned the energy to pull on her clothes and walk down the hall. She took them off again, turned the rusty knob, and stood under the tepid stream in the metal stall. Why was she going tonight? The thought of the phone conversation made her cringe against the mildewed shower curtain. The image of her sitting in a seedy nightclub with the brothers East made her want to run out to the pay phone and call the whole thing off. But maybe she'd electrocute herself on the wires! And she owed Benjamin something. The water drilled against her back, massaged her shoulders, swirled over her breasts, soothed her thighs.

She dried off and returned to her room, wanting to smooth herself into some silk stockings, anything to forget. She pulled on a pair of nylons and a vintage, 1930's cocktail dress she'd bought at a used clothing store on 14th Street, made up her face, and rushed out of the Delroy a half-hour late.

* * *

Benjamin scowled at the art deco spaceships stenciled on frosted glass behind the bar. A superannuated combo played "*Stardust*," the song that had taken this penthouse club soaring forty years before. Benjamin felt nostalgia for the room that had aimed at the stars and been frozen thirty stories off the ground. The last time he'd come was for his farewell party before leaving for Brazil. Fifty close friends had shown up, and many a champagne glass had been raised in toast. What opportunities had beckoned to a young man who'd already conquered New York?

Benjamin lifted his scotch to the future tense of the past, drained it, and ordered another.

Amy entered as the band struck up "Stormy Weather." Through his cups, Benjamin glimpsed a bare-shouldered woman in black velvet negotiating the galaxy stairs. He thought he was flying backward through time. For a moment he was in 1939, his black hair parted on the side, a pencil moustache raking his lip, watching an old girlfriend weave toward him through the tables.

Amy saw Benjamin staring into space and waved, wondering where his brother was. She rushed toward him.

Benjamin couldn't remember her name. He gaped at her like a fool.

"Aren't you going to ask me to sit down?" she said, her soft Southern accent carrying him back.

"Amy!" He pulled out her chair.

"Sorry I'm late. Where's Louie?"

"He was too stubborn to come. I didn't think you were going to make it either. It's almost eight. I've got an early bus to catch tomorrow." With that off his chest, he remembered his manners and fiddled with a white box under the table. "Here, put this on. You look half naked."

"A corsage!" she cried. Nearby diners turned in their seats.

To squelch the outburst, Benjamin resolved to pin on the orchid. But her spaghetti straps presented a logistical problem. His hand trembled with the straight pin, but he managed not to prick her. He sat down, exhausted.

"Would you care for something to drink?" he asked.

"A White Russian, please."

Benjamin thought of the Russian émigrés from the Revolution. He thought of Trotsky, Stalin, the Hitler-Stalin Non-aggression Pact. He wondered what he was doing with a woman to whom history was a sweet drink. But the name enticed him.

"Make that two," he told the waiter.

Amy gazed at the fantasy decorations, the futuristic lamps and cubist ashtrays of an era frozen in highball glasses and preserved in eighty-proof alcohol.

She avoided the eyes of elderly couples. The Stardust Room presented her with a painful vision of aging. The objects remained modern, but the people had lost hair, grown fat, or shrunken and bitter, in their futuristic seats. The blue-mirrored bar reflected the face of modernity. Then she looked at Benjamin, whose blue eyes searched among his peers, strangely vulnerable and open. She had never realized how dated modern art was, yet Benjamin's furrowed face appeared fresh against the gloomy smoothness of the art deco spaceships. He looked almost young. Amy sensed the loneliness of a man who was out of his time. She could understand a little how he felt, because she was a woman out of place. The White Russian made her bold. "When do you leave?"

"I'm catching the six a.m."

"Sounds fun," she said, dismally.

He shrugged and cupped his glass. The coldness of the stars and the thought of the open road made him feel lonely. The orchid trembling on her breast didn't help.

"Found another art school?"

"Nope. I'm still recovering from being called primitive."

"Why don't you go Gauguin?"

"Huh?"

"Come with me to California, where bowers of flowers bloom in the spring, and birdies sing!" The Al Jolson number burst out of him before he'd thought of inviting her, and he recoiled with shame. Amy swirled the ice in her glass and stared at the white tablecloth, her tongue searching her lip. The music blared off-key and shadows of dancers passed over her face.

"Why do you want me to come?"

"I don't like traveling alone."

"Thanks for the compliment."

"All right, you keep me on my toes."

Amy laughed, though her eyes were steeped in sadness.

A waiter hovered over them, and they ordered their meals. Waldorf salad for Amy, and prime rib and potatoes for Benjamin.

"You're not eating. You need to eat," Benjamin watched Amy push things around on her plate like a petulant child.

"I'm sorry Benjamin, I'm just not hungry," Amy forked a broken piece of walnut and put it in her mouth.

"You hardly fill any space as it is, Amy."

"Maybe I don't want to, Benjamin. Maybe I don't see the point. Every hope I've had has turned out to be a bad joke in the end. I don't think I have ever achieved a goal in my life."

Benjamin chewed a particularly juicy piece of beef, swallowed, washed it down with a little red wine. "Nonsense, Amy! When I met you, you had two goals, to get away from Ray, and to come to New York."

"Yeah, and I missed the bus."

"You're not listening! Where are you now, Amy? You're in New York. Why? Because you didn't let missing the bus stop you. You found another way. The same thing applies to your art. You're going to find that success you seek, but by an alternate route!"

Amy put a grape and a little lettuce in her mouth and chewed. The grape was perfect. Sweet and bright against the mayonnaise dressing. "Maybe you're right," she said, and broke into a smile.

She lifted her half-finished White Russian and took a deep drink. A creamy moustache flocked her lip; she licked it off. "I can't believe I'm here!" She reached for his hand. "Want to dance?"

"I don't rock and roll." Benjamin was caught off guard. "But if you'll try a foxtrot." He patted his lips with his napkin and stood.

When she got on the floor, Amy realized she didn't remember the steps.

"Can you waltz?" he asked.

"Yes--"

"Then waltz!" He turned her around in arcs that grew wider and wider, his hand pressed to the small of her back, her hand resting on his shoulder. The spaceships flew by in flashes of glass amid wheeling constellations of stars and fluorescent lights of the skyscrapers glimpsed through the windows. The band launched into *Red Sails at Sunset* and Benjamin felt like a rocket taking off, soaring above the soft cloud of her face, rising to a height above Earth where life seemed timeless.

She held onto Benjamin and felt the centrifugal force throw her cares to the wind like petals from a wildflower. The music spun her around, but she remained still in the center. Her life had imploded in the vacuum of the Delroy, and now it was exploding. She danced. The steps carried her away. She betrayed a smile of far-off places.

A dowager nursed an Old Fashioned and watched the woman in the breath of youth gliding in the arms of faded elegance as the bandleader sang, *That Old Black Magic*. The tuxedo and the cocktail dress glimmered in the pinprick reflections of stars. Benjamin listened to the trombone. The trombonist rode the slide out 'til his arm could stretch no more, to the limits of jazz. A hand muted the horn. The brass sighed like the cold earth at dawn when the wind blew through the jacaranda leaves in the wintry

July of Rio. The bass fubbed the strings of the samba. Benjamin heard drums at sunrise in Copacabana, echoing from a hilltop favela where a party was still on. The singer snapped his arthritic fingers, and Benjamin remembered the metal taps on the heels of a Portuguese knife sharpener scaling Santa Teresa Hill with his wheel and his triangle, calling housewives with his ancient chant.

Black Magic ended and Benjamin shuffled over to the bandleader and requested *Corcovado*. They knew the old bossa nova tune. Amy tried to adjust to the beat, and Benjamin guided her into the mysterious rhythm of Brazil. The whole continent-sized country fit in the sidling step swept between lazy syncopation and the tones of pastels, rich half-tones that colored every bit of sun and shade, leaving nothing black and nothing white, except the undulating mosaic sidewalk that made people dance when they walked. Benjamin sambaed, dreaming he danced with Gisela around the sands of time while the Carioca kites hung bright red in the hazy blue sky, and the faces of the apartments stood still, watching the immutable dance between the American man and the Brazilian woman.

Benjamin stepped on Amy's toe. She jumped, and that was the end of Brazil.

The band went up beat, the toupee'd pianist clinking the keys like ice in a glass. Amy sprang into a be-bop, breaking the invisible bonds of decorum with her hips and tugging Benjamin into the jukebox sock hop in her mind. She twirled and threw her skirts high and twirled back and fell in his arms with a laugh, and rebounded like a rubber band. And she realized she'd come back to herself. She was dancing at the Elbow Room in Harrisonburg, high on Southern Comfort, free as the winds on Massanuttan Mountain.

The White Russian didn't mix with Waldorf salad and dancing. Sweat broke out on her lip, but it was thinking about Ray, not the food, that was giving her cramps. The music changed, and she danced out of his life. She was in New York again, plodding through the streets with her sketchpad and a subway map.

Amy pulled back and shook Benjamin. They danced out of beat, at arm's length, conscious of the eyes watching. Benjamin ached and Amy felt awkward in his arms. They stumbled back to their seats. It was nearly one a.m.. Benjamin straightened up with a start.

"I've got a bus to catch."

"Don't feel bad. I gotta go back to the Delroy."

There seemed no use prolonging the awkward silence. Benjamin insisted on picking up the check. They rode silently down the elevator, back to Earth. He asked where he could mail her a postcard, but she didn't know, and he found himself staring at the stars reflected in the gutter.

CHAPTER 8

"Your tie's crooked!" Lou shouted, splitting the silence of dawn.

Caught sneaking out the door, Benjamin put down his suitcase. Louie swept out of his lair, Dodger blue bathrobe billowing behind him, and stood scowling in the hall.

"Aren't you even going to say goodbye?"

"You were sleeping like a baby. I didn't want to wake you."

"I haven't slept since you came home. Here, let me try that tie." He nearly strangled Benjamin, straightening it. "When you run out of money, don't call me to send you cab fare home. You had your chance, and you blew it!"

Benjamin pulled on his coat and let the tie rankle. He supposed he owed it to Lou to suffer his insults because he was leaving without paying back what he owed from Brazil. But Lou had touched a sore spot.

"I'll pay my debts."

"You don't owe me anything." Louie said, enraged that Ben had converted guilt to gelt. "You're already the loser."

Benjamin glared at his shoes. He wanted to stomp on Louie's bare feet. "Everything is always win or lose with you."

"That's life." Louie waved his naked toes.

"No -- baseball!" Benjamin jumped, missing Lou but rattling the sideboard.

"At least I keep score. I don't hide my errors," Lou sneered.

"So God's an umpire? What about people who don't play the game, who make up their own rules and don't wear a number? Don't shake your head, I'm one of 'em!"

"No, you're just a bum. You pretend other people's opinions don't count, that you can write them off like other people's money. But they matter too much to you. You're ashamed of people seeing you now. Look what's happened to the Big Apple!"

"I don't have to defend myself to anyone."

"Then why are you defending yourself to every Tom, Dick, and Harry? That's why you wrote that *Pearls* tract -- to crib your losses. Mama was right all along. You're a goddamned green tomato. You got picked before you were ripe and then you went rotten."

"She never said that."

"How do you know, you didn't bother to visit her after she begged you to come home."

"And mama's-boy never left the cradle."

The brothers came at each other but were tugged back by invisible hands.

"All right, I'm sorry for bringing Mama into it," Louie panted. "So why did you bother to come back?"

Benjamin's sleepless eyes trembled in the creases of their sockets. He wanted to say, 'To be with you,' but pride held him back. "It doesn't matter why," he said, instead. "The minute I walked through your door you did everything to humiliate me. My whole stay has been an insult!"

Benjamin's pathetic breakdown made Louie turn away. "Maybe I was too rough." He bunched the bathrobe around his shoulders. "I resented you barging in with a dame, and I envied your health." He turned away, the veins in his neck distending and phlegm clogging his throat. "But that's not why I fought you. You were hiding from yourself. I don't care if you wrote a book. You think it's the truth. That's the lie! You don't know any more than the rest of us stiffs about this -- this life." The cough overcame him. He hacked until his face boiled red, and spat blood into a handkerchief pulled from his sleeve.

"Lou, don't get excited. You're hurting yourself."

"I'm not finished." He folded the handkerchief and straightened to his full height, his eyes flashing, his beaked nose raised like a hawk's. "Now answer me. Do you think that book is the truth?"

"Is your batting average the truth? What does the truth have to do with it?"

"Everything," Lou rasped.

Benjamin grasped his valise. "Yes, it's my score," he whispered.

"Not the universal truth?"

"Pearls, baseballs... I guess there's room for both."

"That's all I wanted to hear." Louie squeezed Benjamin to the bones. He slipped a piece of matzo into his brother's jacket pocket. The unleavened bread, the bread of Exodus, was for good luck.

"Write when you get work," Lou growled, repeating the injunction he had used when Benjamin went to Brazil. But he couldn't bear to watch Ben walk down the hall to another folly. He slammed the door and broke into a fit of coughing.

Benjamin took a step down the corridor, wheeled back, and rapped on the oak door. "It's me."

"Go away!" Lou cried.

Benjamin stood, hat in hand, in front of the peephole. "Lou, I can't bear to part as enemies."

"Then stay!"

"I have a small favor to ask. At Miami Airport, Customs seized Gisela's pet parrot, Zazza, and quarantined her like Uncle Simon with TB at Ellis Island. If Zazza survives, you may get a package."

"The answer is no."

"Please forward it to me C.O.D."

Silence. Benjamin stared at the carpet, then turned and walked past the seashell lamps, the trash chute, the frayed red carpet that looked to him like the parting of the Red Sea, and stepped into the elevator. It was his second ride down in six hours.

He caught a cab, watched the bars on the store windows. Lou was imprisoned in Brooklyn, and he was free. So what was freedom worth? He railed at their antithetical fates, yanking the rider's strap. The bars blurred. He knew only that he was here, pushing into the whirlwind of commuters at Port Authority, alone, ignoring the loudspeaker, walking down the interminable corridor to the bus. This aloneness was the only truth. Absolute. Unutterable.

And then he came off the escalator and recognized the orchid. Amy was standing by the loading ramp with the flower in her hair and her back to him, holding her white deal suitcase and a Greyhound ticket. She turned. He gave her a stern look, demanding, "What are you doing here?"

She looked back with haughty independence. Benjamin seemed pale, disoriented. The change in him from last night frightened her. But there was no time for conversation; the bus was about to leave.

"Thanks for coming to see me off," he began.

"See you off?"

Amy threw her suitcase onto the step and climbed aboard, leaving Benjamin staring, dumbfounded at the retreating orchid.

He turned back, hoping Louie would be there. But the cavern showed no sign of his brother. His hands shook and he straightened his hat and climbed aboard, following the white flower down the narrow aisle, past impassive faces, soiled seat napkins, and sea green windows. The bus felt tight.

"Mind if I take the window seat?" Amy said, having already taken it.

"Why didn't you tell me you were coming?"

"I didn't know. I couldn't face another night staring at the ceiling at the Delroy. Besides, you invited me!"

"You have a way of turning up unexpectedly at Greyhound depots."

"If you don't want me to come, tell me straight out."

He stared at her round and direct eyes glinting like the green flash of the sun setting over the curve of the earth. How could he tell her he was delighted, but he couldn't be responsible for her?

The bus lurched from its stall, knocking Benjamin into his seat. Something cracked. He felt his ribs and discovered a shattered piece of matzo in his breast pocket. It smelled faintly of cigar smoke. His throat tightened.

"My brother sends his blessing, a little broken." He passed Amy a piece.

She put the matzo under her tongue -- it felt like a cratered holy wafer -- and closed her eyes. "Please, not another trip to Alaska."

Benjamin turned forward, feeling the unleavened bread melt in his own mouth, and his heart lightened, and the bus bounded out of the terminal into a pothole, startling pigeons into the sky.

CHAPTER 9

Beauty is seeing New Jersey at sunrise from a Greyhound bus through Benjamin's eyes. The rusty piers and warehouses turn rosy as a waking child. Smokestacks shimmer like pink minarets. The outgoing highways are clear, but the heartland pumps produce from truck farms and concrete for construction, as commuter trains rumble through incoming arteries to the boroughs of New York. Manhattan sleeps between the sheets of satin rivers. But New Jersey is up and on its steel-toed boots, bawling: "Gimme a mug a coffee, regular!"

Benjamin gazed out and saw the New York of the '30s that had eluded him in Manhattan, alive and well in New Jersey. He was seeing the world through the rose-colored spectacles of daybreak, framed by Amy's wild hair. She dozed in the seat beside him. If she hugged the window any closer, she'd break her nose, he thought, hiding his smile.

"So long, Big Apple. Here's to you," he whispered. He didn't know if he meant the city or himself. "Hello Garden State, you're looking fresh." It was the orchid he smelled.

Amy's elbow touched his and he shifted uncomfortably in his seat. What would Louie say about her? No, Lou wasn't the problem, he shrugged, turning to the aisle into which protruded the elbows and knees and backs of heads of the bus riders -- a human menagerie. The problem was what he himself thought about traveling with a runaway housewife twenty-five years young.

Benjamin suspected she didn't have much money. He wanted to make a few stops on the way. Smell the roses, as it were. Would he have to fork up for her expenses? It was painful enough having to leave Louie; he couldn't take on another dependent.

Freedom! A whiff of diesel fumes shot through his lungs like a straw, driven by hurricane winds, that pierces a telephone pole. Yes, sir, freedom was what he was looking for. This wingless airplane, this silver zephyr without a dining car, this diesel-powered cattle car with tinted windows and stale air was his chariot to freedom.

He lifted the crushed orchid from Amy's ear. Shifting her position, she leaned against his shoulder, sleeping off her White Russian hangover.

He'd only had a couple of hours of shuteye himself, but that wasn't going to stop him. He couldn't stand to let her sleep through New Jersey. He nudged her ribs.

"Hey, wake up. You're missing America."

She opened her eyes and saw the sky. "Where am I?" Her fingers itched to draw. Maneuvering around Benjamin's knees, she reached up to the overhead rack to get her sketchpad -- and froze.

Crouched in the back of the bus, she saw a man in a cowboy hat, with eyes too close together, staring at her above an upturned whisky flask. Her heart nearly stopped. Ray?

The cowboy saw the wild-haired gal looking at him and broke into a wide grin, showing yellow teeth capped with gold. He swept off his hat, revealing brick red hair and the face of a wasted broncobuster.

"Howdy, want a nip?" he drawled.

She sat down without the sketchpad.

"I thought it was my husband." Her nostrils dilated with a slow exhale. "Funny. I keep thinking he's following me. I called home and my folks told me Ray's saying he's going to kill me and any man he finds me with."

"You didn't tell them who you were traveling with?" Benjamin gulped.

"That was before I knew I was leaving New York," she laughed. "Where are we going?"

Benjamin hesitated, wondering what bomb she was going to drop next.

"Upstate New York."

"I thought we were going to California."

"We are, by the Great Circle route. We've got to see the small wonders of America."

"How long will it take?"

"I don't know." He liked the idea of not knowing. He had cash. He had time. "Maybe a month."

"A month!" she cried. "What on Earth do you want to do?"

He couldn't answer. But with closed eyes, he saw a clear vision. *We'll stand under the stars and wear skyscrapers as coonskin caps and parking lots as moccasins. We'll walk along rivers of highways, tracking diesel buffalo by day and hunting aluminum birds at night. We'll taste the wide-open spaces, climb the Rocky Mountains, and raft down wild rivers to the sea.*

Opening his eyes, he didn't dare tell Amy his fantasies; she might bail out.

"Find a place for my book, and my brother." He forced a smile. "How about you?"

She turned to the window, which reflected her eyes above the fleeting highway. It wasn't Ray who was chasing her. The fears were in her sinews. "I want to stop running and learn to draw." Her eyes turned on Benjamin. "Do you think I'm fooling myself?"

"Am I?" Benjamin smiled beneath his moustache and patted her hand. "Let's get some rest." He closed his eyes.

Amy curled up in the seat, wondering what he meant.

Lulled to sleep by the rocking of the bus, Benjamin dreamed Zazza beat her wings against iron bars and screeched "Socorrrrrro!" *Help!*

"Zazza!" he cried out. The sound of his own voice awakened him.

"Who's Zazza, Benjamin?" Amy asked.

He rubbed the crust from his eyes. "Long story short, she was my wife's boisterous feathered friend. Gisela raised her from a fledgling, spoiled her rotten, and she became an incorrigible squawk-aholic. When Gisela died --" His voice caught in his throat. "I brought Zazza to Miami in a shoebox, but she screeched inopportunely. Customs seized her and put her in quarantine."

"For how long?"

"Six to eight weeks. I feel so guilty."

"It wasn't your fault."

He wrung his hands. "I couldn't leave Zazza in Brazil. She'd die in the wild. Despite her dreadful chatter, I miss her beady eyes and orange beak. She's my last living connection to Gisela." He blew his nose in a handkerchief. "I don't know if she's dead or alive."

"Can't you find out?"

Squinting, he unfolded the Quarantine Release Form. A single orange feather fell into his lap from the folds of the paper. He picked it up.

The print was too small for him to read. He handed it to Amy. "Can you see a phone number?"

"There is none," she said, and read aloud. "'Address inquiries to U.S. Department of Agriculture, Washington, D.C.' Be patient, I'm sure it will turn out."

His chin sagged on his chest. "If Zazza dies, I..."

"And if she pulls through?"

He brightened. "I'll ask Louie to ship her to me in California to squawk in the sunshine!"

Benjamin stood and got his hat from the overhead rack. He tucked Zazza's flight feather into the hat's band for luck.

CHAPTER 10

The Amazon, 1953

They pushed off from the dock before dawn. Benjamin in the bow, Gisela in the middle, and the boatman, Ceará, at the stern of the dugout. The steep banks rose over thatched huts, balancing the city of Manaus under the cloudless copper sky. Everything appeared still on land, beside the two-mile wide flowing highway of the Amazon. But Benjamin's binoculars made the riverbanks come alive with men carrying loads off a steamer and toiling up the muddy slopes. He was well equipped for the journey. In addition to the binoculars, bought at the free port in Manaus, he was outfitted in a khaki safari suit from Harrods in Buenos Aires, a pith helmet, and impermeable boots. It was already thirty degrees Celsius in Manaus -- nearly 100 degrees Fahrenheit by his count; after a decade in Brazil he still made the conversion -- and he was sweating profusely, his cheeks, smeared with mosquito repellent, shone over his neat, black moustache. His blue eyes were cool in his ruddy face, tanned from the beach life in Rio.

The bow edged out into the current and Benjamin looked back and caught Gisela's eyes beneath the broad-brimmed hat shading her face. Are you all right? his eyes asked. Are you sure you want to come? She smiled -- a mosaic of Copacabana beach floating in the Amazon. "Sim, quero ir com você, meu marido." *Yes, I want to come with you, my husband.* Then her lips parted in a mysterious smile.

The boatman primed the outboard and Benjamin saw the dome of the Opera House, built by the rubber barons at the turn of the century. It was a copy of La Scala in Milan: its wrought iron grillwork imported from Manchester, England; its tiles from Portugal; its opera company from Europe. The great Caruso had sung there. The rubber sidewalks rippled in the intense heat. The dome glinted under the sun. The boatman pulled the rope and the outboard Evinrude, imported from Miami, caught on. Benjamin turned forward and the bow lifted and the canoe slipped into the current of the Amazon and headed upstream.

He had been here nine years before, in 1944, in a flying pontoon boat with a geologist from the U.S. Strategic Minerals Program. During the war, Brazil was the only South American country to join the Allies, and Benjamin was hired by the U.S. government for a dollar a year to supervise a Brazilian quartz mine in Minas Gerais, supplying crystals for U.S. military radio and radar. Air-borne, heading north from Belo Horizonte, Benjamin had seen tropical savannah turn into tangled jungle and then an unbroken carpet of green, flecked with blue pools, sometimes rimmed by conical huts of Indian villages. The geologist spoke about the untapped mineral resources of Brazil. Iron, bauxite, topaz, emeralds, petroleum, even uranium, were all said to lie buried in the Amazon. "The man who prospects this region, could be the Sutter of Brazil," he reckoned. As the sun set like a gold doubloon, the plane flew over a native girl washing her hair in the river. The light made her glow as if she were Eve. Then the plane banked and she disappeared.

Benjamin felt under the tarpaulin for the Geiger counter and turned it on. The wind blew the sound of the outboard behind him and he heard, low and crisp like shuffling cards, the clicking of the device.

Gisela looked up, covering crochet needles from which dangled the toe of a bootie, and leaned forward and kissed him. Benjamin stared ahead, anxious. She hadn't told him about the baby until the last day they were in Manaus. All the way up the coast from Rio and on the steamer up the Amazon from Belem, she'd kept her secret. And the day before they left Manaus, with the boatman hired and all the government permission forms signed, she pulled his head to her stomach and asked him to listen.

"Sick?"

"Meu amor, I'm healthy. We're going to have a baby!"

The sun, rising over the banks, sheared off the water, blinding him. It was cool on the river, but his eyes throbbed from exposure to the equatorial light.

"You're getting too much sun," he barked protectively.

"Eu sou a filha do sol." *I'm the daughter of the sun,* she laughed, her voice tinkling over the water like água mineral crackling over ice on the beach in front of the Copacabana Palace. It was there they'd met in the hallucination of Carnival, days and nights drummed into a timeless dance of the samba. He couldn't remember if it was the first or the third night of the four-day celebration. Every night she wore a different costume, every day she sunbathed in the same white bikini. While her parents, wealthy planters from the interior, played at the casino, she'd sneaked away from her chaperone.

Benjamin spotted her on the beach, a tall, tanned woman with blonde hair. She was reading *Gone With the Wind* and consulting a Portuguese-English dictionary. She was different from other Brazilian women, more curious and independent, openly defiant of the conventions observed by the Brazilian upper classes. She saw him looking her over, a foreigner sitting like a fool in a white linen suit and Panama hat on the beach, and she winked. Benjamin was so startled at this Brazilian girl's forwardness that he fumbled, asking the hotel waiter for an ice water in heavily accented Portuguese. She broke in and told the waiter to bring a gin and tonic.

"You understand English?" Benjamin asked.

"A little. Irish nuns teach me *Ingles* at the convent school, but I still learning." She shut the dictionary. "You are going to ask me about the weather, or Sugar Loaf Mountain? I will help you. My name is Gisela." She pronounced it Zhe-say-lah. "I am eighteen and I have many amigos, but no boyfriend," she laughed, covering her mouth. "I can't talk. My father is watching. He hates any man who speaks to me, especially American."

That night at the Teatro Municipal Ball, Benjamin spotted her wearing a costume of sequins and feathers. She was dancing with her father in a tuxedo: incongruous as an Amazon goddess gyrating with a penguin. She gave Benjamin a bold look that, he felt, dared him to follow her. He chased her through the crush of bodies to a moonlit terrace. But when he reached the door, she bolted back to the ballroom and disappeared in the kaleidoscope of dancers. He was about to give up when hands caught him from behind. She pushed him into a snake line, laughing and singing in his ear, pressing her breasts against his back. Until he turned around, and she broke the chain and disappeared.

She reappeared the next day on the beach, in the white bikini, demurely reading *Gone With The Wind*, ignoring him. Then she reappeared that night, at the Jockey Club ball, disguised as a gaucho from the pampas. Benjamin walked by her, trying to act oblivious, and she smacked him with her riding crop. He wheeled, catching her wrist, and pulled her to him. Her lips opened and he felt an inexpressible softness, and then her boot came down on his foot and she ran, laughing, into the dawn. Only to reappear on the beach in the morning and disappear into the night, in incarnations of a Baiana, a Portuguese marquesa, a slave, and then shrugging out of the costumes and lying, without makeup, on the beach.

He approached her with a hangover on the morning after Carnival and stood like a fool above her, holding a glass of soda water; not knowing what to say. She lay in the sun, studiously ignoring him. He turned, seeing eyes watching them from the hotel balcony, and tripped, spilling the ice water on her back.

"Bobo!" she cried. "You silly fool."

"I'm sorry."

"Why don't you stop tormenting me?"

"I like it too much. But I am going away."

"Then what should I do?"

"Ask me to meet you here next year."

The ice melted and she stared at him with the eyes of the night naked in the day. He wrote her letters on Jockey Club stationery, and she replied with wildflowers pressed between the pages of romantic missives. Seasons passed. He visited Minas Gerais on business, and they met surreptitiously. In the January heat, her family moved to their summer home in Petropolis.

One Sunday, Benjamin drove up the winding road to the cool mountain resort to meet her family. But her father was put off by the estrangeiro and forbade her to see him again. Benjamin arranged an encontro at an ice cream parlor with mirrored walls and waiters dressed in white coats. He took off his Panama hat and leaned across the cool marble tabletop.

"I may look like a playboy," he said. "I've had a good time in Rio. But I worked my way up in New York. And I'm going to work again. I'll become the Rockefeller of Brazil. I'll open up the Amazon -- anything, if you say yes."

The boasts made her laugh. But she looked up, and his eyes pinned her, and she knew she couldn't be happy until she whispered, "Sim." *Yes.*

After coded letters, she fled to Rio on a bus, arriving on the last day of Carnival. He met her at the terminal and rushed her to the American Embassy. They were married by the U.S. Consul on the eighteenth of February, 1947. Three tipsy revelers, dragged in from a street band, witnessed the ceremony. The newlyweds donned masks and eloped into the Carnival parade.

The sun, shimmering on the river, disappeared into a whirlpool. Benjamin looked up and saw Gisela staring into the water, adrift in dreams. He wanted to go to her, wrap her in his arms, and tell her he was overjoyed about the baby, but the boatman stood at the bow and pointed to a low, dark island in the distance where the river forked.

CHAPTER 11

"Goddamn dog!" the cowboy hollered at the Greyhound. "Hell, if I wanted to go west on a tractor, I'da taken one, y'hear. A John Deere tractor! Ya stop in every two-bit town and pick up half-a pound of Kotex. Let's go!"

Amy plugged her ears and stared out the window. Three hours and she'd had enough. The seats were so narrow she could barely move. The tinted windows made even morning look dark. The romance of crossing the country had turned into a grim repetition of exits and entrance ramps. Instead of Benjamin's frontier, there was only boredom and claustrophobia.

She resented Benjamin, resented herself for listening to him, resented the world for inventing such things as buses and hopes. Why couldn't they just tell you from the beginning that if you didn't have money you couldn't have freedom?

The bus headed north toward the Finger Lakes, road signs with names from classical literature -- Elmira, Ovid, Ithaca -- and little towns with white clapboard stores and courthouses with cannon balls piled up in front. Then out into the countryside again. Ramshackle farmhouses, weathered and cheerless.

Harvest season had passed, giving the orchards a melancholy look. Benjamin closed his eyes, conjuring up apple trees blossoming in the springtime of 1931. He could almost smell the blossoms. But the only odor in the bus was the nauseating smell of disinfectant from the W.C. mingled with cheap perfume, cigarette smoke, and the faint whiff of undisposed diapers.

A baby wailed. They had stopped in Binghamton and picked up a woman in a ratty fur stole and spike heels, holding a screaming infant. The mother wore a bracelet engraved, "Darleen ♥ Doreen." Nobody had wanted to sit near them, so the mother started to carry on, wiping her eyes one moment and yelling the next, until Benjamin found her a seat. She thanked him for being the last gentleman in the world.

"Nice baby," he cooed to the purple-faced infant. "Pretty blue eyes. Just like her mama's."

The mother, Darleen, smiled. "She usually is. But she's got colic."

"Look at those tonsils. Great lungs," Benjamin said. "Maybe she'll be an opera singer."

"Will you shut the fuck up!" the cowboy hollered.

Benjamin squinted at the fellow in dungarees swigging a bottle of Southern Comfort. He'd been raising hell for two hours, and now the tone was getting mean. The other riders turned away.

"You're bothering the lady," Benjamin said. "Would you please be quiet?"

"Am I bothering you ma'am? Golly, I'm sorry," he belched, waving the bottle. "Don't know what got into me. Just tired of this lonesome ride. Here, give the little critter some Comfort. It'll quiet her down."

Benjamin turned forward, listening to the cowboy sweet-talking the mother. He eyed the other riders. A Marine with a souvenir bag from Times Square. Newlyweds interlacing hands. A fellow with his nose buried in a trivia quiz. A dark-haired student in horn-rimmed glasses, writing in a notebook. They looked like contestants for the refuse-of-your-teeming-shore award. Except they weren't immigrants from the Old World. They were castoffs from the new, fugitives from the breakdown of the family, the new migrants riding the new steerage vessel -- the Greyhound.

In the paper, Benjamin had read about a presidential commission that proposed putting all the poor people from the Northeast on buses and shipping them west to the frontier -- the Sunbelt they called it. Maybe they were right. He felt a painful kinship with the people who "go Greyhound," because they don't have a car or can't afford to fly. He saw the riders stretching out of the depot, back to the low-ceilinged apartments and locked factory gates of the eastern cities, shut down by the recession. And he saw the lines boarding buses and blurring into the white lines of the interstate highways. It was easier to shift people around the states than to fix blame for what had gone wrong in America. But he preferred being part of the westward stream of travelers, even the lost and ragged castoffs, to being marooned with his brother, and his own memories of Brazil.

* * *

Tad's Apple Cider stand flashed by on the road, arousing Benjamin from melancholy thoughts. "Amy, let's get off."

"In the middle of nowhere?"

But he had already stood up.

"Benjamin, what are you doing?"

"I'm getting off." He pushed forward. "Stop the bus!"

The driver looked at the red-faced passenger and pointed at the plaque above his seat.

"It's against the rules."

"It's an emergency!"

"I could get fired for this," the driver complained. But he pulled over and punched the hydraulic door. Benjamin clambered down the stairs and shot outside, his feet slipping on the gravel, and ran back fifty yards to the stand. It was on Route 90 about thirty-five miles east of Batavia, about two in the afternoon.

"Who owns the orchard?" Benjamin asked the little girl in charge, wondering if he'd recognize the name of the grower.

"My daddy."

"Ever heard of the Garden of Eden brand?"

She looked down at her sneakers and shook her mop of curls.

"Benjamin, come on. The bus is waiting," Amy said, panting behind him. She'd left her suitcase on the bus and pleaded with the driver to wait.

"Tell them I'm bringing some for everybody."

Benjamin purchased two jugs of cider and a three-pound bag of apples and lugged them back to the bus.

"Yow-ee! God bless America!" whooped the cowboy.

When people saw Benjamin had homemade cider, everyone wanted some. Facing a riot, the driver checked his watch. What the hell. He backed the bus to the stand and opened the doors. The riders piled out and stood by the road and drank cider and smelled the apples rotting on the frosty ground as the sun streamed through the leaves and the wind riffled their clothing.

The baby squalled at her mother's breast. Benjamin tried giving baby Doreen a little apple cider. She took a sip and made a face. But Darleen thanked him and Benjamin filled the bottle with cider. He squeezed the baby's cheeks and made goo-goo sounds. The baby spit up on his tie.

"Cider, shit! I got something that'll grow hair on your chest," the cowboy hollered, toting a twenty-pound Mexican watermelon from the bus. He sliced it open. The juicy red flesh gave off an intoxicating odor. He'd been injecting it with vodka since they'd left New York, and it reeked of 86-proof alcohol.

The Marine took a slice and smiled, recognizing the peculiar taste. The Latinos and the basketball player and the journal writer lined up. Soon chins were dripping and bellies were warming up as the vodka seeped into their blood. They stood in a circle, their breath rising around them in clouds. They munched and told dumb jokes. They acted like friends. They asked for seconds.

The cowboy sidled up to Amy, standing at the edge of the circle.

"I saved my juiciest slice for you."

"I hate watermelon."

"Well this ain't no normal melon, it's imported from South of the Border. It's got magical powers."

She took a slice, and he asked, "How come you were giving me the evil eye?"

"You look like someone I know." She turned away so as not give him an opening. But the melon tasted so queer and the alcohol hit so fast, she didn't care anymore about Ray or California or where she was going; the tension in her shoulders relaxed and the wind blew her hair and she felt connected to the circle of riders eating watermelon by the road. Maybe that was all she was looking for, nothing grand like Cooper Union, just to be together with people on the way to somewhere.

The cowboy lurched off to try his luck with his second choice, Doreen. First, he had to get in good with the baby. "Hey, little nipper. This'll warm your gizzard."

Watermelon juicing up her lips, Amy found Benjamin standing in the orchard behind the shack.

"What are you thinking about?" she said, smacking her tongue.

He shook his head, lost in reverie among the barren branches of the picked trees. He tasted the watermelon and closed his eyes. "I was remembering when I bought orchards like these during the Depression. Wanted to corner the apple market. I called them 'Gardens of Eden.' Power of a name. Advertising."

"What happened to them?"

"I sold them off."

"Do you have any left?" she said, swaying.

"Maybe one or two."

"Where?" she belched, covering her mouth. "'Scuse me."

He seemed not to hear, but munched, dripping pink drops in the dust. The vodka warmed his blood and he felt again the infinite possibilities of a man of twenty, buying up orchards.

The cowboy tossed the gutted watermelon up in the air. It landed with a squishy thud, spraying seeds.

"I'll find it somewhere," Benjamin said, licking watermelon juice off his moustache.

CHAPTER 12

The Rio Negro, 1953

"The meeting of the waters." Ceará, the cross-eyed boatman, spoke impassively, pointing to a fork in the river.

Ahead, Benjamin saw the black waters of the Rio Negro churn into the white waters of the Rio Solimões. The waters swirled like the tail of a dragon in a Chinese brush painting.

"Senhor, which river?" asked Ceará.

Benjamin looked at Gisela, to see which she wanted. The Solimões was the more settled river, but it was less promising as far as minerals. The Rio Negro was more promising for minerals, but also more treacherous and remote. She looked longingly at the Solimões, the sun lighting her hair like the filament of a lantern. Then she turned back and saw the disappointment in her husband's eyes.

"O Rio Negro," she said.

The boatman obeyed. The Geiger counter clicked and the outboard threshed the black water, impenetrable to fathom, clouded by sediments that promised riches along its banks. As they passed the island, a flock of crimson and turquoise macaws took off, swooping low over the water. Manaus and its opera house now seemed as unreal as Rio had seemed in Manaus, as distant as New York had seemed when he first arrived in Rio. Benjamin felt drawn up the river as he had once been drawn to apple orchards. He came forward and kissed Gisela, feeling her round tummy, and the boat nearly overturned.

"Que engraçado," Gisela stood up, tipping the boat, and stripped down to her white bathing suit. The boatman lowered his eyes from this shameless display of immodesty by a Carioca. Then, just as she was about to dive in, he caught her arm.

"Não, senhora."

"Por que?"

"Piranha."

He pointed to the water and Benjamin saw a school of small fish circling in the shallows. They looked harmless enough, but the boatman took out a piece of dried jerky and dropped it in. Tiny jaws sheared the surface, devouring it, and the water boiled with teeth and tails and greenish eyes. Gisela sat down.

"A selva não é a praia da Copacabana," advised the boatman. *The jungle's not Copacabana beach.*

In the silence of the siesta, Benjamin listened to the cicadas buzzing in the jungle. They sounded like a hidden Geiger counter. The Amazon jungle stretched for a thousand miles in every direction, a frontier larger than Europe, but no one knew what riches lay beneath the green carpet. Gisela was asleep and the boatman was impenetrable behind his crossed eyes. Benjamin climbed down the gunnels, leaned under the mosquito netting, and touched the hardly perceptible swelling under Gisela's swimsuit. The river was placid and the fragrance of orchids drifted down from the trees, and the insects buzzed with the intensity of a continent crying *Eureka!*

"Do you hear it?" he asked her. She nodded, shifting in her dream.

A pirogue paddled by two men in tattered khaki uniforms came toward them from the bank. Benjamin had heard of pirates on the river, but the fragmented words reaching him in the bow commanded him to show their papers to the local delegado. The official was not on board, but rather made his office in a hut floating on four fallen trees from which the branches had been cut, at the end of a bayou.

A dozen barefoot children, the girls in baggy cotton homespun and the boys carrying slingshots, stared out from the gaping window of the raft house. A woman thin as a split beam, with gaunt cheekbones you could hang laundry on, fiddled self-consciously with her rag dress and tucked her hair under a scarf. This was the delegado's wife.

The delegado was waiting inside. Benjamin leaped from the dugout onto the bobbing dock and helped Gisela off. They were led into the back of the raft where an ancient man in grey trousers and a straw hat dozed in a hammock. He jerked to his bare feet when they entered, thrusting his calloused hand into space, and smiling from a face pocked as the river in a rainstorm.

Only then did Benjamin look into his opaque eyes, white with cataracts.

"The gentleman and lady are foreigners." The blind delegado spoke with antiquated cordiality. "I am obliged to inspect your papers, if you please."

Gisela intervened, explaining she was Brazilian and they had received permits in Rio and Manaus. But the delegado insisted on going through the formality, which he accomplished by rubbing his fingertips over Benjamin's passport and feeling the seal. Satisfied, he proudly pulled out his commission, a browned paper folded in quarters, from which a faded ribbon dangled like a lady's garter. He bade them sit down.

The delegado ordered his wife to bring out his best cachaça. She came forward with an uncorked bottle of the cane liquor. He toasted Benjamin, and Benjamin felt the aguardente burn his throat and kick his stomach.

"How far are you going up the river?" asked the delegado.

"How far does it go?" Benjamin said.

"The Indians say it goes to the beginning of time, where the waters flow out of the heavens. But the maps say it ends in Peru. "

"Do you know of any minerals on the river?" Benjamin asked, listing the names.

"Yes," said the delegado.

"I remember when I was young, the river bottoms were full of aquamarines as beautiful as the eyes of your wife."

"How do you know her eyes are blue?" Benjamin asked, astonished.

"All foreigners marry women with blue eyes."

"You're a very wise man."

"No, I am only old and blind, so I can see what was invisible to me when I was young." He turned to Gisela. "My wife tells me you are with child."

"Yes."

"Would you like to stay here while your husband goes up the river?"

"Obrigada."

The delegado smiled. "In Brazil, when we say thank you, we mean no. It is a strange country, no?"

"A fantastic country!" Benjamin gushed, feeling the aguardente. "If my people only knew what was here."

"Perhaps it is better to keep it secret." The delegado leaned forward and cupped the cachaça. "Up the river, you will find a village. If you can make friends with the chief, he will tell you where these stones are, if they are in the matto. But you must promise not to hurt the Indians."

"Of course, why would I want to hurt them?"

"It is not malice. They have no protection against maladies of the white man -- even grippe."

The delegado reached under the mat, felt around, and pulled out something that shimmered white in the hut, a beaded necklace. "This is for your wife. It comes from the berries of a bush that the bruxo uses to heal wounds. We call them perolas. It is more valuable than all the jewels, because it is fragrant."

At dusk, they left. The blind delegado waved, puffing a cigar Benjamin had given him. The odor of burning manioc wafted over the water. Women sat on mats, pressing poisonous juice from the white root, or grinding it in a stone mortar, their babies sleeping in slings on their backs, or throwing grain in brown bursts in the air, winnowing farofa, the staple of their diet. Parrots streaked, chattering, through the trees, their feathers dipped in the colors of the sunset. In an elbow of the river, naked boys flashed brown, diving for fish with wooden harpoons.

The days blurred. Squalls came, raising the river into a torrent. Then, without warning, the rains stopped. One afternoon, in a bend in the river, they saw a village.

Thatch huts on stilts emerged from a grassy bank shaded by wild bamboo. Two people sat on the dock, a smooth-faced Indian of about eighteen, and a younger girl, her hair falling down her back almost to her waist. They were naked except for a penis-sheath and a short grass skirt. As the boat bearing a white man and woman approached, they stepped shyly from the dock. Children squealed out of the huts and crowded the bank. An older man holding a long bamboo pole -- Benjamin later discovered it was a blowgun -- split the crowd and came to the end of the landing. He greeted them ceremoniously.

"Welcome Padre," said the Indian. "We have been waiting for you."

Ceará, who had learned a few dialects, translated into Portuguese.

"Tell him that's nice. But how did he know we were coming?" Benjamin said.

Ceará passed on the message. The chief gesticulated angrily.

"He said he was waiting for the padre to come in the boat and marry his daughter."

"Tell him there's been a mistake. I'm sorry, but I'm not a padre and I can't marry them. But I'm happy they're getting married."

The chief listened and shook his head, crossing his arms. The missionary, who'd lived with the tribe for years, had convinced the Indians they were living in sin and were damned to burn in an eternal fire. The Indians had remained suspicious. The padre said he would come back to marry the youths in a Christian wedding. But he never returned.

"What's going on?" Benjamin asked.

"You're going to do the honors, Padre," said Gisela.

"But tell him I'm a Jew!"

"He doesn't know the difference."

"Then I'll give them a Jewish wedding."

She smiled, humoring her husband. Being married to him was like living in a foreign country, a Brazil where possibilities bloomed like bougainvillea.

He didn't do anything the normal way. He had to do it his way. Like coming up the river on a dugout. Who in their right mind would take a canoe up the Amazon to prospect for minerals? A Brazilian would never do this. Other foreigners would mount a huge expedition -- experts, equipment, and supplies. But Benjamin wanted to be as close to the riverbanks as he could be. It almost made her jealous, his love for Brazil. Standing on the bow, he'd look up the river with eyes full of longing, as if he were searching for some lover in the matto.

In the days of their honeymoon, he couldn't get enough of her. But since they'd come to the jungle, his desire had fallen off. Was it the baby? A pang twinged her belly. It was only three months, but she could feel the baby growing inside. It was foolish of her not to have told Benjamin until they were on the river, but she didn't want to be away from him; to lose him was her fear. She had been so happy when he'd let her come, but a part of her resented that he hadn't cancelled the trip when she told him about the baby. She slipped her arm through his and hugged him, watching the natives prepare for the wedding.

The bride and the groom walked hand-in-hand to a ceremonial clearing by the river. The villagers gathered around them in a circle. The couple bowed their heads. A shaman performed a ritual purification. In an ayahuasca trance, he peered into their eyes and breasts and stomachs, searching for demons. As he cast out each demon, the villagers killed it with spears, shouting and stamping. Then the chief dipped a giant dried gourd in the river, chanted a few prayers, and poured water over the bride and groom. The villagers sang softly. The maiden passed her hands over the brave's body, touching his eyes, his lips, his chest. The brave passed his fingertips over the maiden's body, caressing the eyes and lips and breasts. The shaman slowly revived and rose like a bird, flapping his arms.

The couple returned to the village for the "Christian" wedding. The bride wore a white cotton shift embroidered with butterflies; the groom a store-bought shirt. Benjamin didn't feel like putting on a phony wedding but the chief insisted. Benjamin didn't have a Bible, let alone a Jewish prayer book, so he used the only book he'd brought, *One World*, by Wendell Wilkie. For a traditional Jewish canopy, they used a woven palm mat, held by the four brothers of the groom. Benjamin tied the corners of a handkerchief into a yarmulke, draped Gisela's shawl over his shoulders, and faced the bride and groom under the palm mat.

It was late in the afternoon and the sun filtered through the towering trees, sending beams of light onto their faces. Benjamin bowed his head and recited the Shema prayer in fragmented Hebrew, feeling guilty for playing hooky from his Hebrew classes as a boy. Then the words came back and he recited the prayers, his voice rising to proclaim, "Hear O Israel! The Lord is our God, the Lord is One!"

He must have looked lost, because Gisela pointed at her wedding ring. He remembered her standing, white and beautiful, in the American Embassy in Rio, a photo of President Truman hanging crooked on the wall.

He didn't know the wedding prayers in Hebrew, so he ran through the prayers he'd recited for his bar mitzvah in 1921, at the synagogue in Brooklyn.

The bride repeated the words and Gisela came forward and took off a cheap ring her father had given her and gave it to the groom and he put it on the bride. Benjamin pronounced them man and wife. The villagers stirred with satisfaction.

"Now kiss each other." The Indians looked up, uncomprehending.

Benjamin took Gisela in his arms and kissed her. He saw the Indians out of the corner of his eye and he thought proudly if he could perform a wedding in the

Amazon, he could do anything in Brazil. Gisela trembled in his arms and then his strength came through his lips to her lips and shoulders. And she felt calm again, that he loved her more than the jungle, more than Brazil. And she was willing to follow him up the river, to where the water flowed into the sky, or Peru, or wherever he took her.

CHAPTER 13

A my slid open the window and leaked air into the bus. First thing she knew, they were skirting the shore of Lake Erie. She sat up, exhausted and sweaty. Her head needed clearing and she wanted to change clothes, but not in the filthy bathroom. She looked around. The cowboy had passed out and the rest of the debauched revelers were dozing, a snoring cacophony of watermelon dreamers. She took a towel from her suitcase, tied one end over the luggage rack, and tucked the other in the armrest. The wind riffled the towel. The high seats blocked her off in a little beach cabana between the window and the towel, warmed by the afternoon sun coming from the south.

As she was pulling out deodorant, she heard Benjamin stir in the seat beside her.

"I'm gonna freshen up," she said, hiding behind the towel. "Hold down the ends, will you?"

"Here?" Benjamin grumbled. He looked around for another seat but they were all occupied by sleeping bodies. The only person awake except the driver was the fellow in horn-rimmed glasses, writing in a notebook. Benjamin held the towel, trying to make himself inconspicuous.

Amy turned her back, pulled off her blouse, and let the sun touch her breasts. Lord, it felt so good. The deodorant stick hung unused in her hands. She lounged, impulsive and defiant, bare-breasted on the bus. Arching her back, she stretched her arms. Her nipples stiffened and she touched them with her fingertips. Gently, she smoothed her bruises, still not healed after three weeks. She caressed her sticky flesh. She was tired of talking, tired of hearing about the Garden of Eden and worrying about where she'd be tomorrow. She was tired of drawing on bouncing art pads and fogged windows. She was tired of being afraid. She just wanted to feel herself, for one moment. The towel billowed.

The bus lurched.

In the mirror above the driver's seat disembodied eyes stared at the pale-skinned woman touching herself.

"Benjamin," she called out, covering her breasts with the towel. "I--"

But his head was thrown back against the seat and his chin was thrust forward. The lines smoothed out on his forehead. Color rose in his cheeks. The vodka had knocked him out. He smiled to himself with eyes half-closed.

In his mind's eye, he saw a girl beckon to him from behind a billowing veil. She stared at him with strange earthly eyes, the gauzy towel tinting the bare fields green. He was led into a garden that looked like the Amazon, only everything grew in rows, like a farm. He hesitated, feeling naked before the extravagantly attired plants. Where was his hat?

The girl squeezed his hand and nestled unashamedly. She was sensuous, as Gisela had once been, young and lithe, and she changed shapes as she moved: he could not see her face. Her perfume was intoxicating. He inhaled and felt himself floating on apple blossoms. Where am I?

At first he thought he was in heaven. The bus had crashed and he had been sent to Louie's celestial rendez-vous.

But the bewitching girl shook her head. He looked down and saw she was naked. A snake coiled under his fig leaf. Benjamin gaped. He was in a garden. Eden beckoned, fresh and unspoiled.

He smiled in his sleep, dreaming of Eve. Her body was statuesque, her skin pale green, her limbs sinuous as the Amazon. She floated on her back, breasts buoyantly breaking the surface of the water into golden coins. He had been searching for her all his life but had never possessed her. She was Eve and the Amazon and eternal youth rolled into one! He caressed her breasts of apples, the orchard of her pubic hair. He was young again and strong. She touched him and he sprouted a seed that grew into a tree that fruited in the autumn, bearing apples in its boughs. Would someone pick one?

The Greyhound droned, crossing the state line from New York into Pennsylvania before sunset, then crossing from Pennsylvania into Ohio after dusk.

One by one, the riders awoke from their drunken stupors and rubbed their reddened eyes and aching heads.

From the backseat, stifled cooing sounds were heard as the cowboy and Darleen groped in the dark, trying not to wake the baby. They were just about to get down to business when the bus hurtled over a bridge and descended toward downtown Cleveland. Baby Doreen woke up and let out a scream.

Benjamin shuddered awake, expelled from the Garden into the Cleveland bus terminal. It looked like hell, with pimps wearing sunglasses and pay-TV fires aglow. His head ached. His body felt like he'd been run over by a truck. His empty stomach howled for food.

"Don't sit down, we've got to hurry," he yelled to Amy, who was sinking into a seat, a bandanna pulled down over her forehead, her suitcase stuck between sprawling knees.

She opened a dark-ringed eye. "Where are you taking me now?"

"I'm hungry. There's an all-night diner across the street."

"You go. I'll wait for you here."

"And miss the delicacies of Cleveland? You can't see America without tasting the victuals of the people's diners, a vanishing breed --"

She plugged her ears. "I'll go, on one condition, Benjamin."

"What?"

"That you don't mention the Frontier or the Garden of Eden again ... At least until I get a full night's sleep in a bed with sheets."

But he had already opened the door and was running across the pavement, his valise glowing in the orange neon light of Harvey's Number 1.

CHAPTER 14

Upper Rio Negro, 1953

The Rio Negro branched into a river without name, the river of hope.

The rainy season had come. The six-day journey had taken six weeks, and still they hadn't reached the mineral deposit described by the delegado. The boat had overturned in a storm, swamping their gear. Gisela had swum to the bank and Benjamin had salvaged the Geiger counter, and Ceará cut his leg on the propeller. They had wasted many days huddling in a lean-to by the swollen river, swatting at clouds of mosquitos, watching trees and islands of earth sweeping down the churning waters. Then, as quickly as they had come, the rains stopped. Benjamin wanted to continue. But Gisela refused to go any farther. Ceará, his leg swollen, agreed to stay with her a few days while Benjamin went up river alone.

Benjamin clutched the crudely carved paddle, dug into the water, thrust backward, pulled it out of the swirling eddy, switched hands, dug into the water, thrust backward, paddling up the gloomy river in the predatory jungle. He didn't think, just paddled, his hands blistering and then popping, and the skin rubbing off to raw flesh. It was the second day of non-stop paddling and he was feverish. The swelling on his arm from mosquito bites had gone down, but his tongue and insides swelled instead. Malaria swept into his body, microbes spawning in his blood and sending chills down his spine. In his fever, he thought he saw a young girl, her hair black as the Rio Negro, beckoning from the bank of the river then running away as he approached.

He hated himself for leaving Gisela behind. But he was obsessed. He could not return to Rio without finding something in the jungle. He kept paddling. Beyond this bend, or the next, or the next, there might be an outcropping of emeralds, a radioactive deposit, a seepage of oil... anything, he told himself.

The canoe made its way up the river to a tangled maze of undergrowth where it narrowed and a path began. Benjamin tied up the boat, climbed on the slippery bark of a fallen tree and teetered to the end, where another fallen tree connected, and then another, a chain of trees leading into the jungle. In his fever, it looked like an Amazon highway.

An aquamarine, or was it the reflection of the sun flickered in the water? Parrots took off, chattering, and the jungle echoed with mocking laughter. He crept, then walked, then ran from tree to tree, following the reflection skimming in the water.

He broke into a clearing and halted. Was he hallucinating?

An immense aquamarine lay in the creepers. The odor of the shell necklace rose from the earth, a fragrance of crushed flowers and steamy humus. He knelt down in the moss to pick it up. A snake darted from the undergrowth. He felt a stabbing pain then the cool stone, like ice in his hands.

He awoke with a sharp burning sensation on his legs. He opened his eyes and saw a snake slither away through the grass. The stone was gone. His body felt like it was on fire. He lifted his head and found he was lying on a mound of earth, his knees buried in an anthill. Inch-long ants streamed from the mound and swarmed up his legs, their red bodies flaming. He tried to scream but ants leaped on his tongue, sinking pincers into the tender flesh. He rolled over, crushing dozens under his body, and climbed to his feet. Afire, he crashed through vines to the edge of the river and dove into the water, trying to extinguish the pain. But the water only made the bites blister. He crawled out and rolled on the bank, covering himself with mud.

He came to at dawn, his body swollen nearly twice its size.

His legs throbbed and his heart beat like a drum in his ears. He hallucinated that he was being hunted by Indians. The drumbeat approached and he crept into the leaves and started to run on all fours. He was a jaguar and a hunter and the dart from a blowgun entering his flesh.

The drumbeat subsided and a steady low clicking awakened him the second time. He was still burning but the fever had died down and he could stand on his feet. He followed the sound through the jungle, past the ant-hill to the river, where his canoe bobbed on its rope teth-er. He realized, with a shock, he had gone in a circle no more than 1,000 yards in diameter.

The Geiger counter was making the clicking sound, loud and steady. Either there was a radioactive deposit in the vicinity, or the device had also been stricken with fever. He no longer cared, for the Amazon had reduced him to a savage struggling for life. He switched it off and the clicking continued, mocking him. It was cicadas.

It was easier to paddle downstream. The river carried him swiftly and surely, carving piles of driftwood, which vanished in the backwash. A strange peace fell over the jungle. The trees glowed under the setting sun, toucans skimmed the water, their reflections panning over the mirror-smooth surface. He leaned over the side and washed himself. His face, shimmering against the blue reflection of the sky, was gaunt and contrite and almost human. He dreamed of Rio, settling down in a bungalow on the beach in Ipanema, sitting on the front porch with Gisela, rocking the cradle.

She lay in a hammock, her face flickering like a mask in the firelight. He ran up the embankment and buried his face in her belly, and she winced and pulled his head up, running her fingers through his hair, tugging his beard.

He cupped her belly to his cheek and kissed the life growing inside. She winced again and pushed him away.

"Não, meu amor. É tarde." *It's too late.*

"What do you mean?"

She pressed his head against her belly, flat as a deflated balloon.

"Perdi o anjinho." *I lost the little angel.*

The return journey was silent -- no motor, no words. Weakened by the miscarriage, Gisela lay in the bow of the boat; Benjamin paddled in the midsection, Ceará steered in the stern. They passed the Indian village. The dock was empty, the huts abandoned; a famished dog howled at the water's edge.

"What happened?" Benjamin asked the boatman.

"Não sei. Talvez foi a praga do branco." *I don't know. Maybe the white man's plague.*

He remembered the delegado's words.

The sun rose before them now, and black water flowed beneath the dugout as they were swept downstream by rains, or stilled by the noonday sun. The trees looked somber, the flowers grotesque; even the birds' calls were despairing.

After a fortnight, they reached Manaus. The dome of the opera house glinted in the sun. But they found it rotting on its rubber pavement, surrounded by beggars and brothels.

He paid the boatman and thanked him for taking care of his wife. Ceará smiled though his eyes held sadness. Gisela held out her hand and squeezed his and his eyes seemed to uncross. But it was the angle of the light reflecting off the river.

Benjamin put his arm gently around Gisela, guiding her to the hotel, but she stormed ahead into the bar and ordered a bottle of whisky, the most expensive in the house. She guzzled it like water.

"Come on now. You've had enough."

She looked up with dagger-point eyes, hiccoughed, and started to cry. Picking her up, he carried her to the room, laid her on the bed, and kneeled beside her. He pressed his head to her belly and shivered in the heat as cicadas screamed.

"We're young," he whispered, stroking her hair. "We can have another baby."

CHAPTER 15

A my went to the ladies' room, leaving Benjamin in a booth, facing his reflection in the window. It was 10 p.m. and they'd been on the bus since six in the morning. The overhead light showed exhaustion in his puffy, sleep-creased face, embarrassment in his testy manner, disappointment in his bloodshot eyes. He bent over the table and sighed with feelings that rose to the surface then dove out of reach. His suit was rumpled. Watermelon juice and baby vomit spotted his tie. The seat of his trousers was shiny. There was a telltale spot on his fly.

He shuddered. The trip had triggered fantasies he couldn't control. The emotions stirred up by this skinny waif made him feel like a prehistoric mastodon thawed out after 5,000 years.

The diner comforted him. Harvey's was outfitted with stainless steel coffee machines, Formica counters, and swivel stools with vinyl covers. It smelled like bacon and coffee, echoed like a bowling alley, and looked like an airstream trailer that had grown tailfins. Harvey's served falsely advertised, synthetically treated, artificially flavored, innutritious food to customers who knew exactly what they were getting and relished every bite.

A few of the travelers had wandered over from the depot. Darleen and the baby took one booth. The cowboy headed back to a pinball arcade. The journal writer sat at the counter. Nobody spoke. Hangovers had driven them apart. Amy came back and Benjamin shrugged and avoided her glance. He couldn't face her after having that fantasy. "So what did I do so terrible -- Dream of Eve?" he shrugged. "I should be proud of myself." He felt cursed, doomed to wander in the cold.

The fluorescent bulbs tinted Amy's skin yellow and highlighted the rings around her eyes. She felt a combination of exhaustion and speed, exposed before the plate glass window. She creased the paper placemat, hating the compulsion to draw. She didn't understand why Benjamin was so distant.

"What's wrong? You're acting like a stranger."

"I'm a little groggy."

"You sure were restless in your sleep."

"Did I do something, ah--"

"You were mumbling Portuguese and hugging the armrest. I was going to wake you up, but I passed out."

Thank heavens, he sighed with relief. "Did you sleep well?"

"Horrible. I had a nightmare about Ray. It was the same old thing. I better get to California fast."

"You need a square meal, that's all."

"Coffee?" asked the waitress, splashing brown water into their cups. "Rosemary" was printed on a plastic tag on her breast. She ran a liver-spotted hand through her dyed strawberry hair, pinned under a fairway-green waitress hat. A touch of vanity sparkled in her crinkly eyes, still robin's egg blue after 70 years. "Cream?"

"Black." Benjamin needed a strong Brazilian cafezinho to cut through the vodka residue, but he'd settle for Folgers.

"Please," said Amy, queasy and unable to think of food.

"You better eat something." Rosemary's sisterly tone hinted that Amy looked like hell while sympathizing with her hard travels. She prescribed "melba toast with honey" for the pallid girl.

"Nothing." Amy turned her nose up at the waitress.

"You sure you don't want something else?"

"Yeah, some fresh air." Amy got up and made her way outside.

Rosemary winked at Benjamin. "What's eating her?"

Benjamin shrugged and sipped the warm brew. "I think she's tired of traveling."

"How long you been on the road?"

"Sixteen hours."

"Looks like sixteen days! Where'd you come from? Don't tell me, you're from New York and she's from somewhere down South."

"Virginia. How'd you guess?"

"I ain't been serving coffee for thirty years without learning a thing or two about travelers. I seen just about everything. It's amazing what people let on to total strangers. I should charge for listening. It's gotten so I can tell ahead of time what they're going to say. There's just six or seven stories, and all the rest are variations."

"Which am I?"

She cocked her head and narrowed her right eye. "I'd guess you're a pensioner heading west to Sun City. You've either lost your wife or you're divorced. This girl is some kind of fantasy of youth. You're a safe older man."

"Baloney! You've read too many romantic novels."

"No, I've met too many traveling soap operas. Working the night shift at Harvey's is like watching daytime TV without the commercials. It's one tragedy after the next -- runaways, deaths, abortions, you name it. The bus brings 'em in and carries 'em away, and all I got to do is pour coffee and collect tips."

"Aren't you going to ask me about myself?" Benjamin said.

She wiped the counter. "You're gonna tell me anyway, go ahead."

"There's not much to tell," he said with false humility. "I survived boom and bust on a couple of continents and wrote a book. I'm heading to the West Coast to find a publisher."

She narrowed an eye. "I thought all the publishers were in New York."

"That's the way it used to be." He picked up his coffee. "But now they're moving west. Hollywood. The Human Potential movement. The frontier."

"What's the book about?" she said. "Don't tell me, it's the story of your life."

"How'd you guess?"

"You know how many people come in here with diaries? Look over there," she motioned with her shoulder at the student in glasses writing in his notebook. "You'd think the Greyhound bus was a library. But tell you the truth, I never seen one of them books published. I think they're all running from something."

"What?" He pushed his valise under the counter with his foot.

"Theirselves! The bus is a way to pretend you're going somewhere, when you're just rolling across the country like a hobo on a freight train."

He squirmed in his seat, fighting the urge to tell her about the bums he hired in the Depression to sell apples.

"They're not hobos; they're voyagers, pioneers--"

"And you're Daniel Boone! Why don't people face it, there's nowhere to go anymore. It's one highway with one diner from coast to coast. The rest is just a come-on to sell tickets and keep Greyhound from going out of business."

"What's wrong with a come-on if it keeps people looking for something more?"

"More what? It's fine for you to head out to the wild blue yonder at your age, but what about that girl? Do you think she can afford to end up broke with a man twice her age? I hate Greyhound with all my blood and guts."

"She's free to get off whenever she wants."

"That's not freedom, that's desperation." Her voice dropped. "Don't turn around, your friend's looking."

Amy saw, through the reflections on the glass, Benjamin and the waitress chewing the fat like two old cronies. She could tell the waitress was talking about her from the way she covered her mouth with her claw when she spoke, her neck jigging like a gabbling hen. It bothered her that Benjamin was listening. No, it was deeper than that. What does he think of me?

She glanced up. The student was watching her. He raked his hand through his dark hair and gnawed his pen. She looked at his eyes. Had he seen her undress?

Rosemary went into the kitchen and Amy came back.

"What were you two talking about?" she asked.

"Life in a diner." He avoided her eyes.

"I hate this place. Can't we go?"

"Watch your fingers, the plate's hot," Rosemary said, clattering a steaming platter between them.

Amy took one look at the soggy pancakes, went to the jukebox, punched the loudest song she could find, and danced, oblivious to the diner and the seedy customers.

Benjamin buried his head in his hands, listening to Rosemary complain and avoiding thinking about where he was going tomorrow. That was a long way off. If he started thinking about one tomorrow, he might wonder where all the other tomorrows had gone.

CHAPTER 16

Rio De Janeiro, 1962-1980

"You can't keep a good woman down," he used to whisper to the empty bed, waking up at dawn to find Gisela fixing weak American coffee. He refused to drink her cafezinho, half espresso and half sugar; wouldn't he ever become Brazilian? She'd stand by the propane stove in her shift, barefoot on the Portuguese tiles, the birds singing from their cages on the roof of the bungalow, waves crashing on the beach of Ipanema. And he'd see the halo of her breast and the arc of her hip swaying; and it would hit him: she's still beautiful after ten years, eyes deeper, cheekbones higher, lines giving character to her lips, which never turned down, even when she sang the melancholy samba: *"Tristeza não tem fim, felicidade sim..."*

"Where are you going today, Benjamin?" she asked, always making his name sound exotic, Ben-jah-meen, like a tropical flower.

"I've got a meeting with a man who wants to sell me a refrigerator factory."

Her lips turned up derisively, "Made in Brazil?"

"That's the idea. National industry. It's a beautiful little refrigerator, runs on propane. And it's cheap enough for people to buy. I've already got a name -- Geladeira do Povo." The People's Icebox.

"Where are you going to get money?" she asked, giving a cautionary scrape of the griddle. She'd learned to ask questions before, not after, he launched into a venture. Benjamin had good ideas. He was ahead of his time -- like that idea to import the first TV to Brazil; he'd taken it around, but nobody understood because then there was no station to broadcast a show. But he needed a skeptic to caution him, and she'd become one.

It wasn't just because of him, she shook her head, cutting the pao branco, the horrible white bread he insisted on eating toasted. It was the skepticism of her loins. Two more miscarriages since she'd come back to Rio. Years had passed without her getting pregnant. They'd consulted fertility doctors who said it was her, not Benjamin. After many painful treatments, she'd given up on medicine. In desperation, she'd gone to a macumbeira who performed African witchcraft to cast out the demon. After that, they'd given up on children.

Now she took the crumbs from the bread, climbed up the ladder to the roof, and opened the cages where her toucans and parrots squawked in the ocean breeze. She had her birds, perching on her shoulders, picking at her ears and hair -- hard little kisses. She petted their feathers and looked out at the sweeping crescent of Leblon Beach with Dois Irmaos Mountain, which resembled two brothers, rising from the foliage.

She was happy. Life with Benjamin wasn't what she'd dreamed of. But it was rich and free -- like the wind and the sea and the white beach where they walked every night, hand and hand. He never looked at other women, unlike most Brazilian husbands. Her friends were jealous of his devotion. Ever since they'd come back from Manaus, he'd worked hard in the import-export, giving her presents and attentions to try to make it up to her. And he had made it up! She didn't have children. But she had Benjamin -- her husband and child -- and this was enough.

"Where are you going to get the money?" she repeated.

"I forgot to tell you. Louie wrote, he's offered to help me out."

"We should visit him... and I want to meet your mother," Gisela said.

"I'm not going back until I have something to show -- like this little icebox."

"But you don't know nothing about ice boxes -- or factories."

"I know about the market. This is a natural. It would be like being Henry Ford --"

She slammed the griddle. "Nossa Senhora!" *Holy Lady.*
"Then you're telling me no?"

"You don't understand the word," she sighed, wanting to avoid another fight. She'd tried stopping him from investing in the Brazilian stock market; she'd tried to tell him the partners in the hotel in Gloria were dishonest. But he hadn't listened, had lost all the dollars he'd brought to Brazil, and even had to sell some properties in the States. What could she do? Maybe once he'd be right and she'd never forgive herself for stopping him.

"Get out of here," she shouted, pulling down her lower eyelid in a silent expression of skepticism. "Olha." *Watch out.*

He didn't heed her warning. Brazil was having a business boom. He toured a refrigerator manufacturing plant located in the industrial zone. The compact models were inexpensive compared to foreign imports. The owner, an elderly Portuguese, wanted to retire and move back to Lisbon. He offered the plant for a rock bottom price. The potential market for Brazilian-made refrigerators was growing. Wholesalers promised Benjamin orders. It wasn't like venturing into the Amazon -- it was a going concern, with plant and employees. He'd described it to Louie, with a few embellishments. Lou agreed to co-sign a loan, on the condition that he be paid back in five years. Benjamin changed the Yanqui dollars on the Brazilian black market at an advantageous rate. He paid $35,000 cash, a lot of money in those days. And he was in the re-frigerator business.

It was 1962, the era of great hopes of democracy and development in Brazil. The modern architecture of the new capital, Brasilia, drew international acclaim. Yet the immense cost of constructing the city nearly forced the country into bankruptcy. The government printed money, creating a wave of inflation. Food prices soared so high common folk couldn't afford rice and beans. Economic strife sparked political unrest. Benjamin tried to stay out of politics, but got swept up by destructive forces beyond his control.

Gisela always met him at the gate. He would come home after dark, bringing some doce de goiaba and she would take his hand, knowing from his expression how the day had gone. She would rush in to finish dinner, and he would run down to the beach and plunge into the waves to revive, floating on his back under the Southern Cross. They would eat on the veranda and after dinner, he would sit at his desk, jotting down ideas and throwing them into an old shoebox.

The situation grew worse in 1963. He was selling all the refrigerators he could make, but the delays in payments from distributers caused a cash flow crisis, making him sell the 1952 Plymouth and mortgage the bungalow.

One day Gisela met him at the bus stop with an opened telegram. "Benjamin, your mother --"

"Let me see it." He read Lou's terse words, "stroke, unconscious" and sank with guilt.

"What do you mean?"

"I never went home to see her. I kept postponing."

Gisela walked back to the house and began to pack his bag. "It's my fault."

"What are you doing?" he burst in.

"You go now. I'll run the factory while you're gone."

"Don't you see?" he cried, shaking her. "She won't recognize me. It's too late." He didn't have enough cash to buy the air ticket.

Benjamin threw himself all the harder into saving the factory.

The crisis came in 1964. He was a month behind in the payroll and the creditors demanded payment; but he'd sold a shipment of refrigerators to the government to put in village health clinics. He took the credit signed by the Ministério da Saúde and set out at six in the morning to get cash.

The Bank of Brazil had closed its doors. Armed guards ringed the building. He went from bank to loan shark to Jockey Club, borrowing to meet the payroll. He finally got the amount at five o'clock and was rushing to the factory when a mob halted the bus. It was impossible to get through and he was afraid of being robbed of the bankroll. He turned around and walked from downtown to Ipanema -- six miles -- through crowds of shoving torchlight marchers chanting contradictory slogans.

He reached home near midnight. Gisela had fallen asleep by the gate. She opened her eyes, swimming in moonlight.

"Are you all right? I was worried you'd been shot. There's been a coup."

"Who took over -- the Communists?"

"No, the military."

He took off his hat and slumped by the fence, looking at the bungalow, which would now be repossessed. The moon shone on his bald spot. His moustache was grey, and his cheeks sagged.

"I've got some hot rice and beans."

They went inside and sat by the radio, now playing martial music, and listened to the colonels announce the glorious revolution that would save Brazil from Fidel Castro. Free enterprise would develop the country.

"It's over." He switched off the radio.

"Por que?" her eyes pleaded *why?*

"They'll open up Brazil to the multinationals."

Gisela watched him trace circles in the black beans. It was the first time she'd seen him give up without a fight.

Benjamin wrote Louie, asking for more money, but he didn't hear from him again.

The revolution spawned ten percent economic growth, but Benjamin's prophecy of failure was self-fulfilling. He kept trying. With each new venture, he printed up stationery. Benjamin East: semi-precious stones, English-speaking tours, manufacturer's representative, American feature syndicates... until he finally ended up with Jockey Club stationery and an office in the reading room.

Gisela's father died and they lived for a time on her inheritance and then even that ran out. Years passed, indistinguishable as the headlines of inflation and devaluation, meandering as the River of Doubt.

* * *

Day dawned on the eighteenth of February, 1980, their thirty-third anniversary. Gisela awoke to the chattering of birds and looked at her sleeping husband. Where had the years gone?

Benjamin awoke more animated than she'd seen him since losing the factory.

"I met a man at the Copa yesterday," he told her at breakfast. "From one of those think tanks in America. He says he's got an idea to light up Brazil with electricity."

The color had come back to his cheeks, now crisscrossed with broken blood vessels, and his eyes were quick as the kites darting on the morning breeze.

She looked at the sunburned crown that had uprooted his once black hair, leaving a few white tufts above his shaggy ears, which grew larger as he listened less, his talk becoming a monologue of bitterness. Brazil was a banana republic. Multinationals were taking over the world. He blamed everyone else for what had happened to him, closing his eyes and ranting to whomever would listen, until even his friends at the Jockey Club shunned him. She was the last person he had to berate.

No, he blames himself, she thought, sipping her morning juice. That's why he closes his eyes. But it didn't make it any easier to listen or to see him grow old and disappointed. So she took refuge at breakfast in pineapple juice stiffened with cachaça, and at noon took the first "little red pill," and by dusk, when he came home from his day sitting in the park and writing little notes, which he threw into boxes in his closet, she was ready to hear the whole diatribe: How Brazil had disappointed Benjamin East.

"How is he going to light up Brazil?" she asked, putting her chin on her palms the way she used to listen.

"Dam the Amazon!" Benjamin boomed, eyes closed, stretching out his hands to encompass the map in his mind. "Flood the Amazon basin and create a huge reservoir -- then build hydro-electric dams and pump power to light up the continent. He wants someone who knows Brazil, knows the jungle, and understands Yankee ingenuity. What do you think? I've got to meet him for lunch--"

"But it's our anniversary. I planned a little lunch for us on the balcony." She could no longer hold her tongue, as she used to do, but looked down. The innocence she had lost with his failures flooded back in anger. "Look at me,

Benjamin. You always hide from me. Do you see who I am? Once. Will you see me!"

He opened his eyes and blinked. Her bleached hair was black at the roots. Her skin was yellowish and liver spotted. Her high cheekbones were wan. Her nose had become severe, her mouth shrunken, the corners pulled down by a web of wrinkles cascading in loose flesh under her chin. He remembered the first time he had seen this look in her eyes -- of not trusting him -- now she glared at him. And her eyes, which had looked into his and seen his dreams, were glazed.

"You're my beautiful bride." He gently kissed her. "I'll cancel the meeting."

"Go on, we'll celebrate later." She turned away as if slapped. "If you've got an appointment, you better hurry."

He kissed her again and wsinent into the bathroom to get ready, and she went out onto the balcony. Behind the pot of maria sem vergonha flowers, she kept her whisky bottle. Her kimono pocket rattled with the calmantes the doctor prescribed to steady her nerves. Gracas a Deus, with the right drink you could start the drums of the Carnival, and then with the right pills you could slow the beat and watch the parade. Carnival fell on different dates every year -- it was two weeks off --but she wanted to bring back the first one.

She stood on the balcony and looked down at the undulating sidewalk. She could see all the way to the Copacabana Palace. The girls on the beach wore tangas now, and some even went topless. Not like in her day. But the game of the Brazilian girls who sunned in front of the hotel was the same. Catch a tourist. Let him take you away to a foreign world. Tears filled her eyes. How far did I come? All the way to Leme Beach. She took a deeper swig. The big drums began to boom -- traffic on Avenida Atlantica -- and looking at the bright VWs manufactured in Brazil, she thought she heard tambourines -- water dripping in the shower stall. Benjamin had left it on. But she felt a million miles away, soaring like an iridescent butterfly on a float parading down Avenida Brasil with the surdo drums pounding her chest and glittering dancers flashing sequins. The wind riffled her kimono and she climbed up on the parapet to get a better view.

It was all there -- the whole parade. The little girls dressed as princesses. The maids done up as Baianas. The destaque stars with sequin bikinis dancing until sweat beaded on their bare thighs. The old women limping along, their black faces like African masks. Life was a Carnival from dusk to dawn, and in the end, the pompous judges, sitting in the grandstands, decided which escola de samba won the prize.

How dare anyone judge! She tottered on the wall, swimming out into air heavy with humidity -- buoyant, for she knew it didn't matter who won. The judges were bribed. The contest was rigged. So they laughed at Benjamin singing samba in his New York Portuguese accent.

What did they know of how hard he had tried to become Brazilian, how much he loved this country, even when he cursed it. She was no longer jealous, just powerless to help him. How magnificently stubborn he was. Walking along the street strewn with torn streamers the day after their wedding and pledging to make her the queen. And now, so many Carnivals later, a man meets him in the bar and tells him about damming the Amazon, and he believes it -- wants to rush off to the jungle again.

Damn you! Damn me for staying with you! The bottle slipped from her hands and she reached for it, falling end over end through the air. Glass exploded on the pavement below and she reared backward, grabbing the railing. No, I don't want to jump, she thought, pivoting away. I have to get things ready. But she no longer had the strength to balance herself. The height made her woozy. She gagged. Shaking, she started to climb down.

When the blood rushed from her head, she pitched forward, the kimono billowing, blinding her eyes. She felt a sharp crack on her jaw and lay prostrate on the tiles, trying to call out as the parade swirled and the drums grew fainter and fainter until they died away.

CHAPTER 17

The Greyhound bore through the anthracite darkness of the Ohio-Indiana-Illinois industrial corridor. Cloud cover rolled off the Great Lakes, blocking the sun. The new riders had a dazed look. They didn't talk much, or mix with the others.

Benjamin leaned over, convulsed by stomach cramps. His guts churned and sweat shone on his pate. Amy stared out the window at the factories, which loomed out of the grey overcast and then were swallowed up by winter trees. The farther they went into the Midwest, the deeper she retreated into herself. The damp chilled her. She had no job, no prospects. Benjamin's manic display in the diner had struck her with futility. Her passivity and Benjamin's hyperactivity were two sides of the same coin. This trip was going nowhere.

Benjamin gripped his stomach. A snake coiled in his gut and bit at his heart. What was he trying to prove? Just another scheme. But this time there was no Brazil to blame. The bus lurched and he felt he was walking out on the balcony again, Gisela crumpled on the floor. He lifted her. Her eyes were open. He thought she'd passed out. He shook her. She stared through him.

Benjamin stood up like a drunken sailor and groped his way to the back of the bus. Amy watched him sway and nearly fall and finally reach the door.

He held onto the railing, the unbolted bathroom door swinging open and banging behind him as the bus swayed from curve to curve.

Amy tore herself from her lethargy. She found him leaning against the sink, staring at the spattered mirror.

"I don't need -- " he choked.

She came in and held his head as he retched. Water-melon seeds splashed with chunks of undigested pancake in the stainless steel latrine. The stench made her gag, but she clasped his warm head and felt his veins throb behind his cold ears.

"You swallowed that stuff whole, and now it's getting back at you," she tried to console him.

He looked up at her, and his face softened. He re-membered holding Gisela's head, her hair cascading over his hands; he'd kissed the gentle glade at the back of her neck and felt her grow cold. And now Amy was holding his head and he felt her cool hands and there was some-thing about the quiet way she'd come to help. It rushed over him with the clarity of water. There was nothing he could do to bring Gisela back. All the Carnivals were gone and the people dead. Looking at the washroom, cramped and sterile and reeking with disinfectants, something called him with the urgency of a lover -- his last Brazil.

Amy ran water over his wrists. She swabbed his forehead and lips.

"So much for Harvey's," he croaked, squeezing her hand in thanks.

She turned away but squeezed his fingers.

"I'll get a clean shirt." She shut the door behind her and walked to their seats, feeling warm and light, as if she'd broken through a wall inside herself and touched him.

Benjamin flushed the toilet and cleaned up the sink. The bathroom stank, but his intestines were scoured shiny as a copper pot. He panted, purged of vodka and synthetic syrup. Breath purified of dreams and hunger, common breath, pervaded his body. Respiring, moving his limbs, washing his skin, filled him with ethereal pleasure. He inspected himself in the mirror and summoned the courage to leave the bathroom.

Neither spoke after he sat down, but neither had to. Lured by a surreal moving picture, they stared out the window. Give it a chance and the Midwest opens up its Pandora's Box. A gas station unfurled a flag as big as a football field. A hotdog stand shaped like a wiener with its roof painted mustard yellow. Billboards advertised Walkmans, VHS recorders, and something called the

Apple computer. Gizmos unimaginable in his childhood were now transforming America. A tractor towed a pre-fabricated house. A new way of life on wheels had been pioneered while he was wandering around Brazil, and people flirted with personalized license plates and carried on political debates with bumper stickers. Golden arches heralded a new covenant between man and the hamburger. Fast food fed fast everything -- velocity had become a way of life.

But there was another view out the window. The smokestacks of Gary, Indiana, smoldered behind refineries flaring natural gas against salmon-colored clouds. A 16-car pileup turned heads toward white halos punched in windshields, as ambulance sirens screamed the Kaddish of the highway. The evidence of violence, gunshots or cars backfiring, radiated through the bus with the dim glow of taillights.

They were so close to tenements they could have pulled in laundry flapping on lines. Yet the bus protected them like clothes in a dry cleaning bag. They were alone in their thoughts, reassured by each other.

Who lives here? What are their lives like? Questions rose like smoke from chimneys and sailed over the rooftops. Traveling was like staring at a candle. At first it appeared to be just a glimmer, then slowly beneath it appears fire burning in eyes, glowing in rooms, leaping over walls, lighting the sky.

He pulled his book out of his valise and leafed through the pages. This was all he'd rescued from his life. So little, to look at the two-inch thick stack of yellowed paper, bent at the edges, the sheets a little longer than American typewriter paper. He hoped for a bestseller. But today he'd settle for one person to read it and like it, maybe get a grain or two of truth, a wild idea, a smile.

The Skyway Bridge arched its rusting exoskeleton over the Calumet River.

Chicago crouched beside Lake Michigan. The last rays of sun glinted off the Sears Tower, and the Skyway arched its back and clawed at the tenements. Then they were downtown, beneath the screaming El. Crowds slanted against the wind and surged forward, faces wreathed in steam. A traffic cop raised his gloved hand and blew his whistle, unheard and unobeyed, like a *policia* trying to control Carnival chaos.

Darkness. They plunged into the Chicago Greyhound terminal. There was a layover before the bus left for Lincoln, Nebraska. The wind-chill factor had dropped below zero in the Windy City, and all the museums were closed for a local holiday, and the hotel workers were on strike. Because the heating system was broken in the terminal, cross-country passengers were requested to stay on the bus, which was rapidly filling with carbon monoxide. Hankering for escapist fiction, Amy nudged him.

She flashed gypsy eyes. "Read me some?"

* * *

For thirty years, Benjamin had scribbled thoughts on scraps of paper and tossed them into a shoebox in his closet, where they accumulated dust. Spiders wove webs, crickets chirped, moths nibbled, and mice left scat. His fertile imagination spawned fables with allegorical meanings, grains of sand transmuted into pearls of wisdom. On the lonely journeys over washboard roads into the interior, he had conjured up treasures, and lost his shirt.

For thirty years, Gisela had waited faithfully at the gate for Benjamin to return from his journeys. This day the gate was unattended and ajar. He rushed to the cottage.

"Gisela, I'm home!" No answer. Flies buzzed in the kitchen. He ran out to the verandah. Broken glass. She lay crumpled in a pool of blood, the mad parrot screeching on her shoulder.

Benjamin scattered Gisela's cremated remains into the winds atop Corcovado, her ashes swirling around the Christ statue and dispersing over the hilltop favelas. He returned to the cottage with a mop and bucket, and came upon the shoebox in the cobwebs; emptied the scat and scraps into the trash. A few screeds fell out. He picked one up.

It spoke to him.

He sat down at the wooden table and wrote by the light of a candle, casting shadows on the ceiling.

He wove a story about a prospector who picked a glittery rock off a slagheap. The prospector fell in love with a beauty he called Aquamarine...

When Benjamin finished, the sun was rising over the devil blue sea. He plunged into the surf and swam, praying the riptide would carry him out to drown, food for sharks. But the tide turned and waves hurled him onto the beach, choking and gasping.

You are condemned to live.

He typed the manuscript on an upright Remington. *Pearls*, by Benjamin East. "To Gisela, who waited by the gate." The random subjects reflected his disordered state of mind; his shattered worldview.

It was 226 pages long, two inches thick, and stained with rings of coffee. He tied it with twine, tucked it in a manila envelope, and slipped it in his carry-on bag. A short time later, he sold the cottage, tied up his affairs, and boarded a Southern Cross jetliner for Miami. And then he met Amy.

* * *

"Whatcha gonna read?" Amy asked. Not really caring. Just wanting to hear his voice, like a lullaby.

"From *Pearls*." He rustled the pages and selected a passage, "'*Sandy Sees the Human's Condition.*'" He cleared his throat. "It's a tall tale of hard labor, big dreams, romance, and talking rocks. The main characters are a prospector, a gem named Aquamarine, and a grain of sand called Sandy."

"Huh?" Amy closed her eyes.

"In the backlands of Brazil, a poor prospector toiled in the hot sun and tropical downpours. He possessed nothing and was reviled by all humans, but the waves sang to him, 'Do not weep, you will slave and hunger and die, but I am with you. I am beautiful. I am free,'" he began in a gravelly voice.

Lulled by his voice and the swaying of the bus, Amy drifted in and out. Wheels thrumming, engine droning, they rolled through Illinois farm country. Telephone lines, water towers, grain silos. A billboard boasted, "Dixon, Illinois, welcomes our native son, President-elect Ronald Reagan."

"*Bedtime for Bonzo!*" the cowboy cursed, lighting up a Marlboro.

Benjamin read on. Motes of dust swirled above his bald pate, wafted by puffs of hot air. With eyes closed, he recited favorite passages by heart, conjuring up a love story between a poor miner and a blue gem, which mirrored his own. He lost sense of present time and was carried back to a fictitious past, as the bus hurtled toward an ineluctable future.

"Sandy sat in the dust before the shack and thought about the human's condition. The human had thrown away Aquamarine, but he had gained the sea."

"Zap comics and Dante!" A wild visage in horn-rimmed glasses popped over the seat. "I mean, amazing allegory--"

Benjamin blinked in confusion at the eavesdropper, not recognizing the journal writer. Amy turned to shield Benjamin. Her body sang with the sound of the human speaking to the sea, and she wanted to bounce the intruder out the window into the reeking stockyards reeling outside the bus. She glared at the young man smiling so eagerly at them. "Read me some more, please?"

The young man sat back, but Amy could still feel his presence. His riveted attention.

Benjamin read on, "The sun was just coming up over the ocean. From the shack, the human could see a hundred miles of ruby sky bending over the sea. A grain of sand caught in his eye, bringing back the loss, and he turned away. The sand fell from his eye. He turned, his knees sinking, and remembered that in his dream he'd thrown the aquamarine into the sea. She shimmered in the waves, unreachable and free."

They had left the terminal in the middle of the story, but Benjamin hadn't seemed to notice they were moving.

The eavesdropper thrust himself between the seats. "I don't mean to invade," he said, shaking Benjamin's hand and introducing himself to Amy. "I'm Joshua... I'm a writer, too. Do you give readings?"

CHAPTER 18

J oshua had shaved off his beard and bussed west from New York, looking for the Great American Novel in everyone he met. He was twenty-two, the author of a novella that began, "It was the day Richard Maverick fell hopelessly in love with the surface of things."

Maverick was a thinly veiled stand-in for Joshua, who was in love not only with the surface of things, but also their color and sound.

"I'm keeping a journal." Joshua thrust out his college-ruled composition book. "Do you critique other people's stuff?"

Benjamin leaned back. "No, I ignore the critics. Just left the pundits of publishing in New York, and now I'm heading out to the Free Speech Movement on the West Coast."

"Really?" Joshua stifled a groan. "I was just showing my stuff in New York, too."

"What did they say?" Benjamin's eyelids lifted like crushed velvet theater curtains.

"Oh, my writing has flashes of brilliance, and my point of view is unique, but basically the book stinks." Joshua forced a laugh.

"So they reject the kids as well as the codgers," Benjamin muttered.

"Have you thought of stopping in Iowa City?" Joshua said. "It's a haven for writers and artists. Maybe I could set up a reading."

"A reading?"

"Yeah, I'll invite some friends, serve wine. You could be discovered."

Benjamin's heart flew up in his throat. He saw a best-seller shimmering in the barren cornfields of Iowa.

CHAPTER 19

The University of Iowa Writers Workshop was an oasis of culture, a mecca for aspiring writers in the heartland of America. Famous authors gave seminars on its greensward and avant-garde poets delivered readings in its ivy-covered Quonset huts. The Writers Workshop was selective, rigorous, critique-driven, insular, competitive, and highly acclaimed.

An alternate writer's colony had grown up on the periphery, attracting rebels, rejects, dropouts, hangers-on and, once in a blue Iowa moon, raw talent. The outsiders had something of an inferiority complex, which they disguised as contempt for the literati. Joshua identified with the Beats, such as Jack Kerouac and Allen Ginsburg, but secretly hoped to be accepted by the Writers Workshop.

The bus rolled onto a bridge, passing a sculpture garden by the river. Benjamin watched Amy as they passed the university arts center. She was totally on. Radiating emotions that would fill a ten-foot canvas. She had no style. She just threw on the paint. And that was the artist in Amy. Then they passed the austere art school building and she shrank in her seat, cut off. This was the wounded Amy who'd run from her husband and been rejected by Cooper Union, and was still running. Then she straightened up, switched on. Benjamin smiled at the whole Amy, on and off. And she smiled back. Just the right smile. And the bus crossed the Iowa River.

As they left the depot, they were shocked by the warmth of the air. It was unnaturally balmy for an Iowa winter and people crowded the sidewalks, enjoying the spring-like evening.

"My place isn't far from here," said Joshua, leading the way. He pointed out rundown rooming houses and cheap diners that he considered proper writers' hangouts on the fringes of campus. "Here, let me take that," he said, reaching for Benjamin's valise. "You must be exhausted."

"Exhausted?" Benjamin shouted, provoking two coeds to gawp. He careened down the street. "What a pastoral paradise to ponder the possibilities of the world. Look at those ivory towers!" He pointed at the sterile science center and admired the ivy-covered halls Joshua yearned to be welcomed into. He read a bulletin board: "Poetry reading, Shakespeare, anthropology lecture, modern dance." He accepted leaflets from a student radical, a campus evangelist, and a fraternity man.

"Great literature must pour out of this thought factory. Eat your heart out Dostoyevsky!" He imagined himself writing in this haven, so different from the lonely room where he'd tapped out *Pearls*. He looked at each face and building and book with the respect of a man without formal education.

"Hey, look who came back," said a voice in the shadows. A pale fellow wearing #4 darkness sunglasses, a lime green shirt, a houndstooth jacket, and checkered trousers emerged onto the path. Joshua sighed, embarrassed, but stopped and introduced them to noir detective writer Raymond Valentine. Valentine gave Benjamin a once-over, ogled the chick, and said to Joshua, "Bedouins from your hegira to Mecca?" He leaned a bit toward the east, a condition prompted more by Mexican tranquilizers than religious preference, kissed Amy's hand, and welcomed Benjamin, whose rumpled suit, Broadway hat with an incongruous feather jutting from the band, and stained Brazilian necktie brightened up campus with the look of a shamus from the '30s. "Bien venu to the cornfields of culture," he saluted them. "Staying long?" He deduced that their presence meant Joshua had failed to make it into the holy Kaaba of publishing and would be self-destructing here for a while longer.

"Yes, well," stammered Joshua. Then he remembered the invitation and blurted out, "Benjamin is going to do a reading at my place tomorrow night. If you or anybody else wants to read, bring your stuff. We got to go." Joshua charged off with Benjamin and Amy. Valentine shook his head, admiring how life mirrored bad detective fiction.

Time seemed to accelerate at a speed inversely proportional to their exhaustion. As they approached Joshua's walkup, they saw a seedy barbershop, a clapboard prayer hall, a package store, and an American Gothic hobo standing in front of an American Gothic church. Benjamin and Amy moved so fast that any moment they'd break the sound barrier or collapse. As Benjamin flew down the street, he saw bright, clear shapes in the blur. Amy was a wonder, half-invented. Joshua was a wonder, a little manic. Benjamin marveled at life, which sped him down a street in Iowa as if to a fire, yet let him see the newness and specialness of each face, fleeting and eternal.

"One second, let me get my mail. Here's the key, let yourselves in. Apartment eight." Joshua mumbled, seeing his mailbox stuffed with self-addressed manila envelopes smelling of rejection.

At the bottom of the stack, he found a letter from a college friend named Cassandra. "Dear Joshua!!!!" He winced at the memory of their one-night stand, which had turned into a crazy nightmare. He'd cut off contact and hidden from her for two years. How had she found his address in Iowa City? He shoved the letter in his pocket.

Amy walked up the two flights, anxious for a shower and a bed with clean sheets. She opened the kitchen door and gaped at the filth.

Joshua had thrown a goodbye dinner for Valentine, minimalist Wright Duke, and three tasty poetesses before flying to New York. They had spaghetti in tomato sauce, garlic bread, tossed salad, and several bottles of Chianti. The conversation had ranged from Hegelian dialectics to .45 caliber ballistics and ended up with minimalist poet Wright Duke rising to his six-foot, one hundred and twenty-five pound slump and reading a poem entitled "Gallons of Allen." It began, "I have seen the best minds of my generation drown themselves in blank verse..."

Duke's poem, which had apparently been used to wipe the spaghetti off the dishes, had grown green mold and spawned several generations of flies. Fleurs du mal bloomed from the salad. A mouse scuttled between Amy's legs, waving its tail at the synthesis of food and literature.

"What happened?" Amy said, holding her nose.

Benjamin charged in, threw open a window, and grabbed a broom. Amy mopped up the filthy bathroom and scrubbed the tub.

Joshua reached the landing and marveled at the two strangers cleaning up his apartment. He couldn't feel rejected with them accepting him for what he was, an intellectual slob. He threw the rejection slips onto the manuscript graveyard in his closet. Cassandra's letter informed him that she was out of the mental hospital (great!), was living nearby (really?) and she wanted to see him (not again!). He threw her letter in with the rejections and shut the closet door.

Amy carried dirty plates past a wall of posters: Allen Ginsberg in an Uncle Sam top hat; Bob Dylan with rainbow hair, Walt Whitman with white beard. Benjamin was mopping the floor. Feelings of appreciation even Joshua couldn't intellectualize tightened his chest.

"Here, I'll do that," He took the sponge from Amy, and as he did, the edge of his thumb touched her pinkie finger and they both felt something flare. He cleaned the whole bathroom with a vigor akin to passion, working up a sweat.

Afterwards, he paused to wipe his brow. "Boy it's almost balmy. Hey," he said to Amy, who was carrying a pile of old newspapers past the bathroom door. "Thanks so much for your help. I really appreciate it." His smile awoke something in Amy that she wasn't sure she was ready for, but it felt good all the same.

"I brought the warm weather from Brazil," Benjamin said from the living room.

"Thanks. Now you two get some rest. Tomorrow morning we've got to put out the word and set things up for the reading."

"You're sure it's not premature? You haven't even read my whole book yet. I'd like to get your opinion."

"I'll read it tonight."

Joshua's low-ceilinged apartment had one bedroom with a mattress on the floor, a yellow plastic mushroom lamp balanced on a cardboard box, books piled up in stacks, leaning precariously. In the living room there was a futon couch, a dinette table, and rickety chairs. The bleak apartment struck Amy with incredible loneliness, echoing her own. She felt a tug of longing, mingled with curiosity, but this also frightened her. She took refuge in a scalding bath that steamed the windows and closed her off in white porcelain silence.

Benjamin turned in early but couldn't sleep. His worries multiplied like fruit flies. He took *Pearls* out of the valise and wandered through the pages, restlessly searching for a chapter to read tomorrow. He gave up and set the manuscript on the table and went outside. Wind blew through the branches of an oak. He stood beside it, feeling excitement kite upward through his ribs toward the crystal stars. What brought me here? *Pearls* will dazzle them! He declaimed a few lines, and a piece of trash skittered across the street in applause

Amy was asleep when he returned, wrapped in a sheet on the futon. Joshua sat in the circle of light from the yellow lamp, reading Benjamin's manuscript. Benjamin ached to know what Joshua thought, but he didn't interrupt. He sat down on the hallway floor. Amy was in the next room, safe and warm, and his book was being read by a writer of the young generation. He had come a long way since landing in Miami. His spirit burned like the sun.

About one a.m., when Amy went to the bathroom, she covered Benjamin with a blanket and saw Joshua reading in the front room. He scowled, abrupt and angry. Despite Richard Maverick's love of superficiality, Joshua was a deep reader. He'd picked up *Pearls* with hunger. He finished the book, empty and sick.

It wandered. It was badly written. But its amateurish faults might have been forgiven. What condemned the book was that Benjamin was asking the reader to take a metaphor seriously for 300 pages.

Why had Benjamin written a fable? In order to draw parallels between the behavior of animals, minerals, vegetables, and the plight of man? Joshua didn't know. But he suspected Benjamin was hiding something from the reader, from himself. As the metaphors multiplied, they blocked glimpses into the writer's soul. The book was written in disappearing ink.

CHAPTER 20

A t 6 a.m. Benjamin awoke, revitalized by sleep, endeared by Amy's peaceful form in the living room. He felt purified and ready for his reading. He tucked the blankets under Amy's chin and tiptoed away. At his desk, Joshua slumped over a dozen sheets covered with handwriting -- a short story he had finished before dawn. *Pearls* lay on the floor, the pages strewn haphazardly. Benjamin felt a sudden premonition. But the baselessness of his fear made him shut the door and embrace the brilliance of the morning. The day of his comeback! He knew it with every bone in his body, as he had known the moment he saw Gisela glittering in the Carnival ball, that he would marry her.

He gazed out the window. Pink light shone on the white clapboard church, played ring around the barber pole, and sang off the wire mesh of the package store. The street glowed, the sky was blue, and the mild weather felt more like spring than winter. Benjamin donned his Panama hat and went wandering into the dawn.

Amy never got to the art center that day, but she passed it, carrying a shopping bag of tequila and junk food that Valentine had bought with food stamps at the corner market. Joshua had slept in, hoping that by over-sleeping he could cancel the reading and forget he had ever read *Pearls*. But Valentine had dropped by, accompanied by Duke, to help with preparations. Seeing him asleep, they'd kidnapped the aspiring art student and got her to spend the whole day with them, knocking on doors, pinning notices advertising "Greyhound Literary Arts Festival" on trees, announcing it on university radio, etc., until about 3 p.m., when they decided to drop her back at Joshua's.

Joshua first heard the news of the reading on the radio, which he promptly hurled onto the manuscript graveyard.

"Jesus Christ, it was just an idea, I didn't mean it literally."

"It's a little late now," Valentine smirked. "Getting cold feet?"

Joshua looked at the floor, where he had flung *Pearls*. His own fear of being exposed before an audience faced him from the little mushroom lamp where he'd written his story. Maybe his first reaction to Benjamin's book on the bus had been the right one. Maybe Benjamin would rekindle the same excitement. Footsteps echoed up the stairs. Two mighty sacks of groceries budged through the door and bumped their way toward the kitchen.

"Anyone for honey?" Benjamin crowed, cracking open a jar. "Best thing to warm up your speaking voice."

Joshua didn't have the courage to say no.

T he Greyhound Literary Arts Festival got off to a start with a volley of beer cans and a cloud of marijuana smoke.

"The first shot," quipped Valentine. "Russian roulette before an audience of Iowa cornballs."

The room was cleared, or rather its emptiness rearranged. The reader would stand before the wall of psychedelic art posters, and the listeners would sit on the hardwood floor, sweeping back to the window.

In the front row, Benjamin sat on Joshua's mattress, which someone had dragged in from the bedroom. He wore a blue serge suit, with a red carnation in the buttonhole. He glanced at the students and nervously shuffled his manuscript. This group of writers in their twenties was as strange to him as the first Brazilians he'd met at the tiny airport of Belem, on the way to Rio in 1941. It gave him vertigo to think of all the people he'd met in his life. He'd tried to disguise them as minerals and fit them in *Pearls*. Would his book be any more comprehensible to these students than the Jewish wedding prayer had been to the natives in the Amazon?

Amy sat beside Benjamin, waiting expectantly for the reading to begin. Joshua stared into the crowd, fidgeting with his manuscript. Finally, the last few straggled in and climbed over people sitting cross-legged on the floor.

A professor emeritus, who'd gone to drink after the death of his wife, announced, "Enough dawdling, dilettantes. Show your stuff!"

No one wanted to begin. Several people had brought their pieces, but realizing they would not automatically get applause and, indeed, might get hooted out, had hidden their writings. Finally, a poet from New York who had made the unfortunate decision to write poems about people, not images, and, what's worse, funny poems that were not parody or farce, stood up, looking thin and awkward, and walked to the front. There he underwent an extraordinary change. While appearing to apologize for reading, he showed the audience it shared his plight and convinced him there was no reason to apologize, because he loved the people in his poems and he wouldn't apologize about them to anyone.

Benjamin sat back and watched an ancient mystery unfold between the poet and the audience -- the mystery of humor between people who take life seriously. When he was thirteen, his father took him to a vaudeville house in Brooklyn. A fat comic in a ragged suit and ridiculous bowtie stood up before a crowd of meat handlers and made fun of himself. They laughed, sharing the verbal blows. Then the comic shifted his tone, reaching out to sadness and love. The poet reassured Benjamin that the practice of the old mysteries had not died.

Wright Duke hadn't intended to read, but the applause for the poet changed his mind. He pulled out a story that had just been rejected by a soft porn mag that was nevertheless so impressed with his talents that the editor wanted him to stop writing fiction and take over the true sexual confessions section. In his slumped, ducal style, Wright read a story about a not-too-bright fellow named Willy who won a radio-sponsored vacation to Dubuque. For some reason, unknown to Wright, the story worked. The audience cheered for Willy at the end.

The Scotch-garbled professor emeritus snorted, as if saying, so what? I came here to hear the great themes of my time: suburban adultery, ethnic narcissism, sexual combat, and female mysticism.

But Valentine was so inspired that he took out of his pocket a monologue entitled "Last Thoughts of Echs" -- a chapter from his detective novel -- and read an incredible, visionary stream of meditations. A shamus and a shaman, a private eye and witch doctor, Echs used sorcery to solve his cases and flatfoot techniques to unlock the secrets of the universe.

* * *

Joshua turned pale as the applause for Valentine died away. He had decided to go next while Valentine read, and he wasn't going to back down now. He strode up to the front and stood like a first-time nude model facing a drawing class. Joshua possessed the sort of bravery that exhibited itself in magnificent acts of private cowardice. To Amy, it was as if an intense light glowed through his features like a Japanese lantern. Bracing his elbows against his sides to stop his hands from shaking, he read the short story he'd written in the wee hours of the morning. The letter from Cassandra had triggered it, but he'd changed her name to Daphne, and his own to Christopher.

He condensed the background story: One lonely night Christopher turned up at Daphne's doorstep. She cooked him green curry chicken and they got drunk on Greek retsina wine. Later, Daphne freaked out on acid, dropped out of school, and went home to Detroit, where her bewildered parents locked her up in a mental hospital. She wrote Christopher a letter pleading for help.

"I visited Daphne in the lockup unit in Detroit," he began. "I wasn't prepared for what I saw. When the white-coated attendant unlocked the steel door, I heard a scream. Christopher! CHRISTOPHER!'

"She came running from the end of the corridor in purple stockings, knees pumping, thin arms stretched wide. Daphne leapt into my arms, sobbing, 'I didn't think you'd come!'

As Daphne rushed toward him through the corridor of fictitious memory, Joshua lost consciousness of time. In the audience, a woman wearing a paisley dress moved slowly toward him.

"Who's that?" Valentine whispered to Wright.

"Dunno."

A few minutes later, Joshua finished the story, to light applause. The woman in paisley broke through the crowd, crying, "Joshua, Joshua, it's me, Cassandra!"

He froze.

She threw her arms around him, aiming a wet kiss at his face. "Aren't you happy to see me?"

Joshua averted his mouth from her lips. "Excuse me, friends," he said, leading Cassandra away.

Amy's stomach twisted like a turpentine-soaked paint rag. Joshua turned around at the door and looked back. Amy thought for a moment that he looked directly at her. Then he was gone.

Amy turned to Benjamin, whose knee jigged like a sewing machine treadle. She touched his shoulder, "Take your turn. Good luck."

* * *

Benjamin stood up to face the audience. Joshua was a hard act to follow. But that was the challenge. If he couldn't reach these kids, who was his book for? Benjamin straightened his tie and peered at the faces before him.

What am I going to read? He'd thought about it the night before but never decided.

That had never bothered Art Tatum. The blind jazz pianist, who'd tickled the ivories at the Essex Bar in the '30s, always waiting for the sounds in the room to tell him the tune. Benjamin closed his eyes. Silence. A tennis shoe squeaked.

The young writers watched this unschooled old man drag out expectation by doing nothing. Benjamin's stage fright threw the audience back on itself. But his stillness also increased the drama.

"This passage is called Mother of Pearl," he said, to blank stares.

Amy saw his worried brow, swallowed her own apprehensions, and gave him a furtive thumbs-up. A frisson of excitement thrummed his heartstrings. "Since his last adventure on the ocean bottom, Sandy was swallowed by an oyster and transformed into a pearl."

Wright shot a puzzled look at Valentine, who knifed the Duke with a dirk smirk.

Oblivious, Benjamin read on, pages trembling in his hands, sweat under his arms, throat growing dry. Minutes dragged on, chairs squeaked, and the audience grew restive. Amy heard voices coming from Joshua's room: Cassandra weeping, Joshua trying to calm her.

What crazy relationship did they have? Color me green, Amy thought, wrestling a twinge of jealousy. What was Joshua like? His friends were weirdly charming, in a bohemian sort of way. So different from Ray and his macho buddies. What would it be like to go to art school here? She needed air, time to think, and couldn't bear to see Benjamin making a fool of himself. Quietly as she could, she slipped out, feeling liberated but guilty for abandoning him.

The professor emeritus groaned. Benjamin's eyes watered, blurring the typescript. "To make a long story short," he said, launching into a seemingly interminable digression.

"Pathetic," muttered the professor.

Discordant voices rose from the back. Benjamin's ears reverberated with their whispers and his eyes swam with tears. He saw Gisela in sequins and feathers beckoning from the first Carnival ball, and then the kimono crumpled on the ground. He didn't see the audience turn away in embarrassment. Several students exited, stifling titters. The maudlin display of an old man weeping had emptied the room.

Someone turned on the stereo in Joshua's bedroom. Marijuana smoke blued the air. Jazz bebopped from a Charley Parker album. The music blocked out the voice of Benny the Dreamer reading the final lines to an empty room. The audience grown restless, had left their seats.

Inside every pearl
Of wisdom
Is a grain of truth.

* * *

At about midnight, while the party was in full swing and Joshua was holding court, Benjamin sneaked out the door. He stood and railed at those haughty baby boomers that didn't know their ass from a hole in the ground. He couldn't distinguish the cold response to his writing from sheer repudiation of his existence. Worse than being rejected, he was irrelevant, shivering outside in the cold. He raged against snot-nosed kids who didn't have the decency to show respect to their elders. What a fool he'd been to bare his soul to strangers. With the help of a bottle of chianti and the darkness, he struggled to regain control of his emotions.

Where was Amy?

He looked for her in Joshua's room, but she wasn't among the boogying partiers. She had left before the end of his reading and apparently not come back. He knew intuitively where to find her, at the art school by the river.

Benjamin steadied himself, for he had drunk too much. He heard an ambulance siren and remembered the cicadas in the jungle. No, he wasn't going to drag Amy down the highway, as he'd dragged Gisela upriver. 'She wants to go to art school, I won't hold her back.' He trashed the bottle and lurched into the cold winter night.

A path led to the river, where the sculptures gleamed in the moonlight. And there stood Amy, silent and motionless as a Pop-Art statue. 'She seems at peace among her own kind, as if she belongs here,' Benjamin thought, retreating cautiously into the shadows.

He stumbled back to Joshua's, apartment, threw his clothes into the valise, tiptoed over bodies entangled on the floor, and pitched out the door.

On the way to the bus depot, he passed an elm tree bearing stars in its leafless crown. *Pearls* was a dead weight in his hand. He waited on a bench with his head throbbing from an incipient hangover. The eastbound bus was due at 12:45. He considered for a moment taking it back to New York. "Hullo, Lou. Here I am again, sorry. I went bust out West. Will you take in your repentant brother?"

But he wasn't particularly sorry. And the westbound bus came first. He climbed aboard, feeling strangely light. He stowed his valise in an overhead rack; relieved of the weight, he sank into a seat, and noticed there were fewer riders in the Midwest.

"Even poor people own cars here," he thought, with unrelenting optimism, wrenching his eyes from the sculptures by the river. He looked ahead, fixed on a shadow receding at the end of the road.

He had thrown away his pearl; now he wanted the sea.

CHAPTER 22

A my heard a stick crack and saw a shadowy figure retreating from the riverbank. Numb with cold, she was slow to react. By the time she recognized Benjamin, he was gone. She felt drawn to the water, shooshing under thin ice, and she made her way down the riverbank, but the warm weather had thawed the muddy earth and she slipped and fell, sliding on her back into the frigid water. She pulled herself out, ashamed, and hurried back to Joshua's. The party was long over.

"Benjamin?" she said, hearing a rustling sound in the dark.

"No, me." Joshua stood, barefoot and shirtless, rubbing his hairy belly. Without glasses, he looked like a satyr.

"I thought Benjamin was with you," he said.

Amy stopped and turned back, as if breasting a wave - - guilt.

"Maybe he wants to be alone after the debacle," Joshua moved toward her.

"No, he needs to be comforted. I shouldn't have deserted him."

"Why? It's better he saw the reaction tonight than to go off to California thinking he's going to sell that book."

"That's easy for you to say. You're great at letting people down. Where's Cassandra?"

"I ditched her."

"You bastard!"

"At least I'm up front about it. I wanted to be with you tonight."

Despite an unfamiliar warmth in her belly, Amy gave in to anger. "You have a strange way of showing it."

"Hey, you're shivering. Hold on, I'll get you something warm." From his bedroom, he called out, "Do you like Iowa City?"

"The sculpture garden is beautiful."

"Is that where you went?"

"Washing my sins in the river," she sang out, finding it easier to talk when he was in the other room. He returned with a towel, a coarse wool sweater, and two red socks. "Thanks," she said, taking them. His eyes, without his glasses, were penetrating, as if he normally carried windows on his nose to peep into the world. Without them, he was exposed.

"What sins?"

"Letting people down. First myself, then my parents, now Benjamin."

"Why yourself?" Joshua asked from the kitchen, "Want some tea? Black, or chamomile?"

"Chamomile's great." While he was in the kitchen, she tiptoed into his bedroom and closed the door. Through the thin wood she said, "I let myself down because I wanted to be an artist. But I got married instead." She hung her head. "I don't know if I married him because I felt sorry for him or because I was afraid to go to New York."

"Do you feel sorry for yourself now?" Joshua lit a meditation candle resting on a saucer, and the fragrance of orange blossoms overcame the kitchen smells. He carried the candle with him.

Amy sat down on his bed, pulled off her blouse, and wrestled the cable-knit sweater over her head. It caught on her wet wrists. "You sure ask a lot of questions," she shouted.

"It's my job." He pushed through the door, balancing cup and candle, and gaped. Her face was covered by the sweater. In the flickering candlelight, her upstretched arms raising her small breasts made her look like a Degas nude, 'Après le Bain.' Joshua rattled the cup, scalding his hand. She pulled the itchy wool half way to her bare knees. He set down the candle on a bedside table, stealing a glance at her. She took off her dripping pants and pinned the sweater between her crossed legs with the steaming cup.

"How did you let your husband down?" Joshua called, having returned to the kitchen. "Sugar or honey?"

"Sugar," she said. "I provoked him and he... "

"Sugar's bad for you," he said. "What?"

"Don't make me repeat it!"

Joshua stopped in the doorway. Amy stared at him with eyes made huge by her pale skin and red hair; and her words became fixed in his mind with the steaming cup before her sex.

"I'm sorry." He sat cross-legged on the bed, facing her.

"You forgot the spoons," she mumbled, to stop herself from crying in front of him. "I'll get them." And she set down the teacup and hopped barefoot into the kitchen, white bottom flashing like a cottontail. She found two spoons and brought them in. She gave Joshua one, sat down and dipped the other in the jar of honey. "I said I wanted sugar," she muttered.

Joshua stared over the rim of his cup at her wrung-out face, and there was something in the bony knees and defiant chin that said she could not be pushed over or torn apart like Cassandra. And her eyes, how could he say it without offending her? They recalled Dylan's 'Sad-eyed Lady of the Lowlands.'

"Tell me how you're a survivor," he whispered.

Amy poked her finger into the candle and rubbed the hot wax with her thumb. The pain made her concentrate.

Her words poured out disjointedly. Joshua was stunned by the torrent. She came to Ray's marriage proposal on Massanutten Mountain, and Joshua's hand moved across the flame and stopped her from burning herself. She looked up. He pulled her toward him. The flame went out and she stopped talking.

As they kissed, Amy smelled the dried sweat that had glued his shirt to his back during the reading. His mouth was still warm with words. Her eyes burned, her breath came short; he confused her fear for passion.

She stiffened when he touched her breasts.

"What's wrong?"

"It's just you're the first since Ray -- "

"Sometimes if you act out a trauma, you can conquer your fear," he whispered. "Open up, let go."

"Are you sure?"

"Trust me, okay?"

She bit her lip, trembling.

He mistook her silence for acquiescence. "Tell me exactly what Ray did."

"He held me down."

"Like this?" He pinned her arms. "Then what?"

"He asked if I had my diaphragm in."

"Do you?"

"Don't touch me!" She hurled him off, rolled on top, and pinned down his elbows with her knees. Enraged, she shouted, "Do *you* like it? Does that make you feel open?"

"I was just trying to help."

"The hell you were. It was turning you on! Just like when you watched me on the bus." She sobbed in darkness, clutching her breasts. Joshua lay with his back to her. After a long silence, she heard him get up. "What are you doing?"

"Writing in my journal."

She pulled up the sheets and raged, "I'm just a character to you, aren't I? Cassandra, Daphne, *me*, we're all grist for the mill." She pulled on her jeans, shot out of the bed, and opened the closet door. Benjamin's valise was gone. So was his hat.

"Oh, Jesus." She hid her face. She'd sensed when she'd come back from the river that he might have left, but hadn't let herself face it. She threw her own things into her suitcase, jammed the lock, and stood up. "If you want to write about people, you'd better stop treating them like characters." She shut the suitcase and pulled on her coat. She wrenched open the door and stood in the hall. "I hope you finish that story. And I hope someone publishes it so the whole world can see what a bastard you are."

Amy threw on her clothes and ran back to the river. The sculptures glowed in the moonlight – cold and eerie. Her fingers clutched the fingers of a dancing girl frozen in bronze. Wind from the river dried Amy's eyes. Benjamin had probably gone to the bus station. She cursed herself for being so stupid. She ran by looming classroom buildings. She passed the bulletin boards and dorms, retracing their steps from the day they'd arrived. She reached the depot with the Greyhound emblem – lights off, door locked. She peered inside: empty, closed until 6 a.m. Amy thought of calling Louie. Perhaps Benjamin had left a message. But if he'd wanted to leave a message, he would have left it at Joshua's.

Her skin appeared yellowish under the sulfur streetlamps. The cheap diners and funky boarding houses were lifeless. She had wanted her freedom and now she had it. She faced the empty storefronts, the parking meters. She was done running.

A car door slammed behind her and she wheeled around.

"Howdy--" The voice came from a shadowy figure in front of a beat-up '61 convertible.

"Stay where you are!"

"Don't you recognize me?" the man drawled, pushing back his Stetson to reveal his greenish eyes.

"Watermelon Cowboy?"

"Yeah, I saw your friend, the old coot, a while ago. I figured you'd show up sometime." He flashed a shit-kicking grin.

"What are you doing here?" Amy rubbed her bleary eyes.

"I've been waiting for you," he lied, taking off his cowboy hat.

In fact, he'd been waiting for Darleen.

He'd had no idea Amy would be at the depot. Three days ago, he'd gotten off the bus with Darleen to visit her sister in Muscatine, on the Illinois border. He couldn't take it anymore, so he pawned his collection of engagement rings for a $495 jalopy. He even let Darleen call him by his real name, Maynard. He was going to drive her to Texas, try shacking up for a while, and they would leave baby Doreen with her sister in Muscatine. But last night Darleen had put her foot down and refused to abandon Doreen. Maynard hemmed and hawed, panic stricken at the responsibility of becoming a stepfather. Darleen took Doreen and got on the 12:00 p.m. bus from Muscatine. Maynard followed her west to Iowa City where he saw Benjamin get on. Pride prevented Maynard from chasing any farther after Darleen. He slept a few hours in his car parked in front of the depot, with no idea of what he was going to do next. Then Amy had turned up.

He pulled out his last cheap ring and launched into a marriage proposal. "Listen, the old cuss is gone. How about us?"

"Don't give me that. What happened to Darleen? Where'd you get this car?"

"It's fate!" He held out the rhinestone ring. "Darleen and Benjamin brought us together."

Amy listened to his rap with a mixture of astonishment and panic, 'til she heard him cry, "They eloped, doggone it! Dropped us like a hot frying pan. I saw it coming for a long time. There's nothing we can do now. We got to pick up the pieces."

"You mean they're on the same bus?" Amy asked, hearing only that. Tears filled her eyes. "Let's go!" she cried, grabbing him and hugging him. "We don't have much time."

"No, we don't," he smirked, hitching up his belt. Did she want to skip the nuptial rites and jump into the backseat with him immediately? He gestured at his car, its aqua tail fins shining in the rusty light of dawn. "Don't you think she's a beautiful honeymoon-mobile?"

"I sure do," Amy shouted. She climbed in, tossing her suitcase into the backseat. "I'm ready if you are."

"Here?" the cowboy balked, looking at the bright streetlights.

"Yeah. I can't wait."

"Well, at least let me put the top up," he argued. "You're liberated, but doin' it in the backseat, folks might pass by."

Amy burst out laughing. The cowboy threw down his hat, jumped on it a couple of times, and kicked it into the backseat of the convertible. "You don't mean you want to chase after that old fossil?" He cursed under his breath. "Goddammit, I want to be with Darleen." He stared at the dashboard and chewed a wad of tobacco, tense and angry.

"I'm sorry it didn't work out," Amy apologized, opening the door. "But thanks for telling me where Benjamin went."

He looked at her with loaded eyes. He spat out the tobacco, switched on the ignition and shifted into first. "Stay in, goddammit. I've seen half-assed women before, but this is the first time I've ever seen a lady riding shotgun on a posse. High ho' silver, hold onto your Tampax. We'll ambush the dog at the pass. And if we're going to be traveling together, you might as well know my name is Maynard."

The bus had five hours, at least 200 miles, on them, Maynard figured. But he had tracked the dog from Muscatine and knew its plates and its route. He could even spot its tracks -- oil stains and ticket stubs. It was a local that followed the old four-lane Route 6 through Des Moines and Omaha, and only rejoined the interstate six hundred miles west near Fort Morgan, Colorado, about one hundred miles east of Denver. Maynard showed Amy the route on the map. He held the wheel with his knee and pointed out an alternative northern route that ran parallel to Route 6, but was a faster eight-lane Interstate. The bus route was more direct, he argued, but every John Deere tractor and wide-load trailer was on Route 6, and the crippled dog wouldn't be able to average more than 45 mph. But on the interstate, they could hit the Chevy's top speed, 68 mph, and wail into Fort Morgan in about ten hours, just ahead of the bus. The disadvantage was they might miss the Greyhound altogether, being on separate routes. The bus fueled up in Denver, the regional depot, and the passengers would board new lines and be impossible to track from there. So it was interstate or bust. With the pedal to the floor, the top down, and the car heater on full blast, Maynard barreled onto the highway.

"You're crazy, dude!" Amy cried, burrowing down in her overcoat. The sun was behind them at 9 a.m. when they crossed into Nebraska and began following the dry bed of the Platte River. Amy hadn't been in a car since the taxi in New York, and she enjoyed slouching all over the aqua vinyl seat, twirling the radio dial, picking up country and western stations, news reports, and storm warnings. The weather was rapidly changing. A National Weather Service meteorologist warned of a cold front bearing down from Canada colliding with a warm front from the Gulf of Mexico. The same front that had brought such unnaturally balmy weather to Des Moines.

"Yahoo!" Maynard whooped.

But as far as Amy could see, the sky was blue, and the heater warmed her feet.

Maynard was a crack driver, especially on the straightaways, but he didn't like to put his hands on the wheel. "Cramps my fingers." He leaned back with the seat at the rear position, the toe of his boot on the gas and the heel on the brake. He steered with his knee, his elbow, his left ankle, and even for a while with his belt buckle, until Amy yelled, "Enough!"

In Nebraska, the wind blew tumbleweeds across brown plains patched with snow. Amy's skin felt parched. Everything looked dry: dry trees beside the dry riverbed; dry stubble fields, and dry roadside signs advertising a place called Little America. Except for its alcohol supply, Nebraska was the driest place Amy had ever seen, and if she hadn't been so cold, she would have told Maynard to pull over so she could pee in the dry riverbed. But they had no time. He couldn't get the Chevy past 68 mph downhill, even when he held the wheel with his hands, and the pistons were losing compression steadily.

They passed Grand Island, the halfway point, after six hours. In the next four, they were going to have to cover 200 miles.

So they began to fidget and rankle and feel utterly mournful, until not even making wisecracks about Little America could comfort them, and they succumbed to that most awful of pursuits, which Americans only resort to when all else is lost, and will cross the whole country to avoid mentioning. They discussed what was on their minds, what they really felt, what they were going through. In other words, love.

"Jesus Christ, I'm married to one man and chasing another old enough to be my father," Amy complained, admitting to Maynard what she had never admitted to herself before. "And I was supposed to be free! I should jump out," she half-threatened, grabbing the door handle. "I'm lucky we won't catch their bus. What would I say to Benjamin? Hello, I'm sorry I abandoned you, but once I was with Joshua, I missed you?"

Maynard listened, steering with his big toe. He waved his cowboy boot in the air. "Goddamn papoose-packing Darleen got a good deal and she blows it for ten pounds of shitty diapers and a doll that cries Mommy. My mother left me when I was a pissant, and look how I turned out. Darleen won't settle for less than me adopting Doreen. Do you believe that? Me! Now even I wouldn't do that to a kid. Why the hell am I chasing after them anyhow?"

Amy asked herself the same question, but she knew the answer for the cowboy. He had found what he'd been looking for, bumming around the country, giving engagement rings to rodeo groupies in every hick town. It was so easy to see in somebody else, so hard to understand in herself.

When she'd reached the empty depot, Amy had felt like she'd finally stopped running from herself. And then the first chance, here she was, following Benjamin. She asked herself why? Was there something inside her that couldn't be satisfied? She looked out at the parched riverbed licking at the road like an endless, unquenched tongue. She looked at the trees that reached out with their branches -- for what? She understood Benjamin's frontier better now. It was a big emptiness that needed to be filled.

"Why do we feel guilty about love?" she asked, watching Maynard play it cool with the steering wheel and biting back another outburst about it. "We don't mind filling ourselves with watermelon or whisky. But people?" And she laughed, because this was Benjamin speaking in her. She wanted to hear him talk up Nebraska 'til it became the Garden of Eden.

But maybe he wasn't so optimistic anymore. Maybe what had happened at the reading made it all different. She saw Benjamin riding, silent and alone, on a bus full of strangers. She missed the smell of his cologne.

The western sky was a huge grey overhanging shelf of storm clouds, fifty miles away. It drove toward them with forking veins of lightning followed a half minute later by thunder. At 3 p.m., they crossed into Eastern Colorado, an hour behind schedule. The cloud shelf swallowed the sun and thirty-mph winds nearly blew them off the highway. The temperature dropped below zero. Thunder echoed from the heavens. Snow began falling before they could get the top up.

Maynard slowed down to twenty mph, steering with his knee, and Amy wrestled the convertible roof over their heads. She found a foot-long hole in the center. Hail stones the size of golf balls banged on the hood. It sounded like a Trinidad steel drum band. Amy used her suitcase as a helmet. Maynard steered past Sterling as the sky darkened to nearly black and the snow and hail piled up in two-foot drifts against the barns and barbed wire fences of Eastern Colorado. The Chevy had no snow tires, to say nothing of treads, and Maynard condescended to skate them toward Fort Morgan with his hands on the wheel. It was nearly 4:30, an hour-and-a-half late, when they reached the junction where the Greyhound route rejoined the Interstate. The Greyhound wasn't there. Maynard parked by the fork anyway. Amy was too frozen to cry.

"I'll bet that storm slowed 'em down," Maynard wagered, shoveling hail out of the backseat. "Let's wait and see."

Not more than a half-hour after they stopped, the cloud shelf fell away, the sun came out, and the sky of the West, bluer and deeper than Amy had ever seen before, shimmered above the snowy plain. From the shredded storm clouds rose shapes like kneeling white buffalo -- the front range of the Rocky Mountains. "Buffalo?" Amy thought. She sensed Benjamin was coming.

"Well, I guess we might as well head on to Denver." Maynard sighed, starting up the car, "I know a great little motel--"

"No. Just wait a little. Look over there!" she pointed. A snowy bus wobbled on the icy pavement of the two-lane Route 34.

"That's our dog!" hollered the cowboy. He gunned straight for the Greyhound on a head-on course. Amy jumped on the seat, stood up through the hole in the roof, and waved her hands at the driver. Maynard slammed on the brakes. The car and the bus skidded up to each other and kissed bumpers.

* * *

Benjamin believed the bus had been halted by the freak storm. Now the sun was shining outside.

"You never know what's happening with the weather in Colorado until you read about it the next day," he told the 75-year-old widow across the aisle, a great grandmother from Broken Bow who was visiting relatives in Salida.

Then that fellow with the cowboy hat got on. Benjamin recognized him from somewhere. It was strange, he could remember that face and associate it with something like watermelon, but he didn't know if it had happened yesterday or fifty years ago. The cowboy walked the length of the bus and stopped before a blonde in the backseat, who was holding a baby. They commenced squabbling and the other passengers gawked. Then the woman stood up and handed the baby to the cowboy and he walked out sheepishly, carrying the infant. She stomped behind, a proud look in her eye.

Passing Benjamin, the baby stuck out its rattle, and Benjamin remembered the cowboy and the woman and the baby were from the trip to Cleveland. Yes, they had all eaten Mexican watermelon by the side of the road. He waved, amazed. The cowboy waved his beat-up Stetson.

And then Amy appeared. Benjamin believed he was dreaming. In the day traveling since Iowa City he felt like he'd spent forty years, growing forgetful and not even remembering a fellow he'd known only a week before. The driver shut the door and started up. Amy was carrying a white suitcase on her head the way women carried water in jugs up the slopes in Rio. Beautiful Baianas, with bandanas on their heads, their bare shoulders shining in the sun. He couldn't remember how long ago he'd seen them. Only that just recently -- was it yesterday? -- he had stood on a cliff in Rio and thrown a stone into the sea. And here now, coming toward him with ice in her hair and her eyes shining like the sea, approached this apparition of Amy.

CHAPTER 23

The hail melted by the road, disappearing as they drew close to Denver. The cowboy honked and drove south. Snow shimmered in the sunset and was gone, a wonder like the new calm between them. They were a mile high on Earth, the last gasp of plains before the mountains.

The bus reached the outskirts of Denver at rush hour. The streets were dirty, but the air had been swept clean. The ugly commercial strip of Colfax Avenue looked, to Benjamin, like a Broadway of possibilities. It took an hour to get to the downtown depot. Amy and Benjamin seized each tumbleweed and neon sign as an expression of the luck of being together. People looked healthier, younger, stronger. Buildings were going up, despite the recession. Old ones were being torn down. History didn't seem to matter here. The past didn't weigh the place down. They stood at the door of the bus station and watched the stars rise over the purple mountains.

188 · JONATHAN FREEDMAN

The next express didn't leave 'til midnight. They wandered around lower downtown, enjoying the hours with nothing to do. Benjamin noticed that people said hello. The water tasted good. The waitress kept filling their coffee cups. There was room to stretch out. The license plates were green and white.

Benjamin pointed out examples of newness, progress, happiness; reflections of the happiness he felt with Amy. He didn't see the Five Points ghetto or the Larimer Street saloons, the sterile condominium suburbs, the Rocky Flats nerve-gas arsenal, the Security Life tower from which, that morning, a college student had jumped to his death

The altitude accelerated Benjamin's metabolism. The building boom made him feel young. The crisp air warmed him. The urban renewal refurbished him. The mirror-smooth skyscrapers reflected his hopes. On the streets, the strange mix of people made Benjamin and Amy feel like they didn't stand out. Eastern cynicism and Midwestern circumspection were replaced by open friendliness. They drowsed in the depot, no longer together by chance. The midnight bus to Grand Junction, Utah and points west was announced. They roused themselves and boarded the Greyhound. The last thing they saw of Denver was the gold dome of the state capitol peeking above the brown cloud.

"He just wanted to use me," Amy mumbled, as the red cliffs of the Front Range closed behind them. Benjamin nodded, seeming to understand whom she meant. "You too," she said vehemently. "We were just characters to him."

Benjamin turned away, considering the two Joshuas -- the talented writer and the inexperienced young man. A faint smile curled the corners of his mouth.

"Don't be too hard on him. He's had things too easy. After he's experienced some failure, he'll be a little more human." Benjamin didn't want to advertise the opposition too highly, so he added, "Until he's had a few knocks, I wouldn't give him a second chance."

"Look, buffalo--" Amy shouted as they passed a mangy herd of government-protected bison grazing beside the road. They came over a ridge and one hundred miles of peaks stretched before them, spiking the sky. The minutes flew; she wanted to slow them down, as if this feeling could only exist in the protected time capsule of the bus.

The Eisenhower Tunnel was closed by a snowslide at the entrance. They lumbered up the old road, reaching the top of Loveland Pass, and it stopped snowing. They were above the clouds. Amy caught Benjamin's hand, and the bus seemed to stand still, for this was the Continental Divide of America, and all the snow that melted on one side ran in streams to empty in the Gulf of Mexico, and all the snow before them melted and ran down to the Pacific. And they would follow.

Then they were over the crest, coasting toward Arapahoe Basin and Frisco, Colorado, as if without brakes, and everything was inevitable, and their fear of what would happen next was eclipsed by their excitement.

A troop of Cub Scouts boarded in Eagle. They reached the end of the Glenwood Valley, red clay rising in a wall of twisted pine and aspen, and the bus crept along a narrow gorge and followed the icy Glenwood River. A silver zephyr of the Denver & Rio Grande appeared, streaking parallel across the river at the base of the cliffs.

The bus sped between eroded shale formations that revealed the geologic record like a book. It was warm and the sky was cloudless, the color of Benjamin's thoughts. Against the prehistoric formations of Western Colorado, the difference between their ages seemed trivial. Then Grand Junction appeared at the end of the valley, surrounded by miles of irrigated fields and orchards.

Time was going faster and faster, the distances getting smaller and smaller, the road seeming to merge into the pearl-white sky.

CHAPTER 24

I can't believe we're getting off in Moab -- Utah," Amy said, climbing off the Greyhound at midnight.

She did a 360-degree turn, swinging her suitcase and scanning the parking lot, gas pump, and diner. Above, the blue mountains slept like Brahma bulls. She could almost hear the stars sparkling. They looked like snow crystals. The wind blew through Amy, through the buildings, through the mountains, as if she didn't exist. And she let the suitcase swing back to earth.

"Benjamin, what are we doing here?"

His eyes sparkled with secrets. Moab had leapt from the map, striking a memory of his bar mitzvah, which triggered a chain of associations reminding him he'd once bought property here. Or had he? It was so many years ago. He wanted to check it out before he told her. "Come on. Let's find a hotel."

Moab billed itself as a tourist town, but people didn't cross the United States to admire this natural wonder.

Moab was a motley collection of temporary one-story dwellings, trailers, liquor stores, and mining equipment warehouses left over from the uranium boom of the 1950s. At the same time Benjamin had made his trip up the Amazon, Moab had already had a few years of radioactive camp-town glitter. Then uranium was found elsewhere and the town lost its glow and stagnated, becoming the haunt of renegade Mormons and aging ore drillers. The raw earth that had disgorged ore to feed America's 'Atomic Café' was spectral, cratered. Yet people were still living in Moab, the neon light on the Uranium Diner blinked, and the oil crisis was bringing back prospectors.

"Feel that energy!" Benjamin inhaled, invigorated. He remembered the iron ore magnetizing the hills of Minas Gerais. He remembered getting drunk one night in Ouro Preto and riding back on a mule under the stars, telling his foreman Jesus about Broadway. He had been in Brazil remembering New York, and now he was in Utah, remembering Brazil.

"It's all connected," he said, rather fuzzily, trying to give Amy an answer why they'd gotten off here. "Everybody goes to the Grand Canyon. But who comes to the Garden of Eden?"

Amy smiled at the words. Symbols meant something positive to him in his private language. She wasn't sure about trying out a metaphor for a vacation spot, but being with him in the emptiness made her feel protected, closer to her past, and less threatened by what she would do in California. She felt invulnerable in this canyon, and memories came back and projected themselves on the red hills carved by wind and water into natural bridges linking earth and sky.

"I think I see," she said. And she took his hand, which was warm as the red brick her grandmother used to put in her bed. She let the sky call up memories and then she let the wind clean them away.

They found the only motel in town with a fourth-story view. Benjamin insisted on separate beds and Amy smiled at his fastidiousness, but was glad to have her own space to stretch out. They collapsed on matching chenille bedspreads, feeling the wonderful luxury of having no reason to be there.

Benjamin awoke alone at sunup, pulled on his tropical weight khaki workpants, and buttoned on a red flannel shirt unused since Minas Gerais. Snapping down the brim of his hat, he strode out into the blue streets, where ice formed in the shapes of the shadows of mountains. Frost crusted the windshields of cars. The temperature was right at freezing, made colder by the wind. But the cloudless sky lay on live coals of the eastern sunrise and warmed him somewhat.

Winter had come late to Moab. Curled under the warm chenille, Amy dreamed of the snows of Shenandoah Valley, when the hills seem half-aged and half-young, patched with frosted dogwoods, fiery leaf trees, and somber evergreen.

Benjamin passed some old Geiger counters gathering dust in the window of a hardware store. His face grew dark as he remembered the rusted one he'd pulled out of the closet after Gisela's death. Before throwing it away, he'd turned it on. The ticking telegraphed the tiny heart stopping, as cicadas keened and faded away. Silence. It was as if he passed the turning point of his life in a window in Utah.

He wrenched away and crossed the street, which was cranking to life. He squeezed between miners in parkas blowing steam out of their beards and women in dungarees walking to their jobs. A single-engine plane flew overhead. He remembered taking Gisela for their 20th anniversary on a plane ride over Rio. They swung around the outstretched arms of the Christ statue on Corcovado, swooped down over the green oval of the Jockey Club racetrack, skimmed over the Lagoa, buzzing bikinis on Copacabana Beach. From the surf to Moab, Benjamin's mind traveled with alacrity. He came upon a display of crystals in a rock-hound store. In 1941, he could have come to Moab as easily as Minas Gerais.

He turned left at a cross street; a tall girl in a white wool coat came toward him. He admired the Utah version of Gisela from beneath his hat. She passed, unnoticing. The sun rose above the mountains and shooed away the ghosts. It comforted him that it was the same sun that roasted the sands of Ipanema Beach and fell in beams in the jungles of the Rio Solimões. Each step of his life had seemed like a leap in the dark, but they had all been taken under the same celestial fire. They all led here to Moab, the great nowhere that reminded him of everywhere he'd lived. Wherever he'd gone, he carried a camp town, boom or bust, in his mind.

He caught his reflection in a patch of ice -- a rumpled fedora silhouetted against the peaks. What am I doing here after all? He half-smiled. He'd pulled Moab out of his hat, but he wasn't showing it to Amy yet. He whistled, anxious to wake her.

Since the reading in Iowa City, Benjamin had grown tired of his desperate need to evaluate his life. He could not just walk through the streets and savor the town as a new experience; he had to make connections to Brazil, weigh the past against the present, unearth memories to prove his worth. He was lost in some vast tabulation of his life that he wanted to complete before reaching California. The constant reflections were wearing him down. The Benjamin who ran up four flights and threw open the hotel room door was in full possession of every faculty, plus one -- the desire to stop remembering and live every moment.

"Up and at 'em. We've got important business!"

"Where are we going now?" Amy yawned, stretching. She stood in her flannel nightgown before the bathroom mirror, unknotting her hair. The dry air made it crackle with static electricity. She'd slept for ten hours. Her eyes were puffy and a crease from the blanket branded her cheek. Her mane spilled like a copper millstream over her shoulders. The sun silhouetted her figure and tinted her face the color of cacao. Benjamin closed his eyes and saw, printed on his memory, an Indian bride standing beneath a canopy. Amy saw him looking at her strangely and closed the bathroom door.

"When you got rejected at Cooper Union, where did I promise to take you?" he called through the wood.

"California," she said, opening it a crack. "Throw me my clothes."

"No, before that," he said, handing over her jeans and sweater. "You told me they called you primitive and I said 'Go Gauguin! "

"Benjamin, I don't want another fantasy."

"It's not a fantasy. It's the Garden of Eden." He stormed out the door. Amy threw on her coat and shoes and ran behind.

"You're looking for what?" asked the property registrar at the County Land Office a half-hour later.

"The Garden of Eden," Benjamin said nonchalantly.

"The deed?" She wanted to tell him it was owned by God, but she held her tongue.

"The property was acquired by the East Apple Company of New York, about 1933," he explained, leaning over the counter, the shoulders of his suit coat sticking out like the cross pole of a lean-to.

He'd had dragged Amy here directly from the motel, kicking and fighting like a tiger and yelling at him, "You're living in that impossible fantasy world."

He'd shouted back, "That's why I picked Moab off the map, because the most impossible fantasy is the one to come true." And now he was here to prove it.

"You're looking for an apple orchard named The Garden of Eden?" carped the registrar. Her eyeglass chains swung in tandem as she looked suspiciously at the red-faced man and the frustrated waif.

Amy turned to Benjamin and whispered, "Is there really an orchard named The Garden of Eden?"

"Yes, but I've never seen it."

"Are you making fun?"

"I am. Of myself."

"Then why are you embarrassing this lady?"

"Madam, does the Garden of Eden embarrass you?" Benjamin asked.

The property registrar's chains quivered like the cords of her neck. Yes, Adam and Eve make me feel naked, her face seemed to say.

Benjamin turned away. All his efforts made people embarrassed. He felt like a trench coat flasher of ideas. The Garden of Eden embarrassed no one in the Bible. But the idea of it existing in Utah! Only a fool or a fanatic would come looking for it in the Land Title Office. Yet it had existed once all over the world. And Adam was a man, and Eve was a woman.

"I bought the orchard in '33, but I didn't keep the papers," he confessed. "Perhaps you could look up the title under my name, Benjamin East."

The registrar walked away, clicking her chains. Benjamin continued explaining to Amy, "Remember, I told you I bought orchards all over the country. Called them 'Gardens of Eden'. Branding. Advertising. Well, they never amounted to much. When I went to Brazil, I sold them off. But this one I saved for some reason. Maybe the name, Moab. It reminds me of the Torah portion for my bar mitzvah when I was thirteen!" he laughed. "'And Moses went up from the plains of Moab unto Mount Nebo, to the top of Pisgah... And the Lord showed him all the land...' How about that? I still remember it."

"It's here!" The registrar's cry rattled the filing cabinets. She stood with the deed in her hand and gave a little start, as if she'd seen a photograph of a streaker. She came back to the desk, holding the deed to the Garden of Eden face down.

"How much is a copy of the title?" Benjamin asked.

"Two dollars," she smiled, her chains swinging like nooses. "But you owe forty years of back taxes."

Benjamin swallowed. "How much is that, more or less?"

"I'll tell you exactly." She picked up a pocket calculator, tapped in the revenue scale and original purchase price, and started multiplying. "You're lucky it's unimproved property in Zone F with a Z tax rate," she concluded, swinging around the calculator so he could see the bottom line in lights. "Only thirteen-hundred."

"The Garden of Eden exists, but I owe thirteen-hundred in back taxes!" Benjamin cried.

He strode out the door, pink revenue slip flapping in his hand, Carnival laughter welling up in his lungs, sweeping Amy into the sky beside him.

Amy gazed at the suit-coated man charging up Main Street. His ideas were so old, almost ancient; he looked like a quixotic knight in rusty armor. He must be freezing in that lightweight jacket and hat on the icy mountain street, she thought. People in wool ski hats and heavy parkas passed them, breathing clouds of steam. The sky threatened snow.

"Benjamin, where's your overcoat?" she shouted after him.

"Who needs it? This is Eden!"

"No, Utah--"

But Benjamin was heading for the orchard.

The address was on the title. He asked directions, and a gas station attendant pointed toward the edge of town.

They turned onto a street where the wind funneled between buildings. The noonday sun shone, as snow crystals flew. Spaces opened up. Bungalows built in the fifties stared blankly from brown lawns. They passed a Silverstream trailer stuck like a grounded airplane. Amy hugged his shoulder. They walked about twelve blocks and still no orchard. They seemed to be going back in time. The facades of miners' shacks gave way to vacant lots. The paved street continued in dirt ruts. A slag pile showed the colored ages of earth.

The mountains appeared like white flowers blooming above the town. Clouds swept above, swift as a herd of deer. She could almost see the cirrus tracks of Indians.

A car whizzed by -- or was it a thought? -- Benjamin wondered, out of breath and aching. His face grew warmer, but he felt chilled. Benjamin had passed restraint and logic. He was so obsessed it was difficult for him to distinguish between thoughts and things. The earth was a blank slate written on by mind -- or matter? The highway was a speeding thought, he believed in that queer logic of excitement. The hamburger stand, slag pile, miners' shacks, each one had begun as a thought -- an idea. On the outskirts of town, fantasy and reality seemed to merge. Garden of Ideas, I'm coming home!

Benjamin faced the orchard he had bought sight-unseen nearly a half-century before. He had picked up his pace and now moved so quickly that Amy was still a block behind.

Fruit trees were one of the first things planted by the settlers. When they survived, it was a little proof of the Promised Land they had sought in Utah. But such orchards were a rarity in the rocky hills and gulches of Utah. They grew only because of zealous care in their first years. A pioneer family had built stone culverts to bring water to the top of the land from a natural spring.

They'd planted a row of poplars, most of them now gone, which had protected the young saplings. The hardy apple seeds had come from Massachusetts. Citrus trees had been planted along with them, but they didn't take, and only one survived. The trees had not been pruned since the descendants were swept up in the Dust Bowl. The land had been auctioned to a broker who sold the parcel to Benjamin East. Except for producing a few dwarf apples, the bulk of the trees had long since stopped bearing fruit. Condoms and beer cans showed what the orchard was now used for.

Benjamin saw a ripe apple through the barren branches at the far end of the property. He crashed through dry leaves, skidded on rotten fruit, and pushed away gnarled branches. The frozen ground crunched under his shoes, and a sharp stone caught in his sock. Thistles pierced his pants. He limped on the uneven slope, a gnarled figure among twisted trunks. A fallen branch tripped him. In his haste, he fell forward, landing on his knees. But he got up; his palms pitted with stones, and brushed himself off. His pants, torn at the knee, fluttered on his aching thigh. He caught his breath and crashed on.

Benjamin had sighted a snow apple -- a nearly forgotten variety. It dangled in the sun a hundred yards away, and in his myopic vision, it looked like the reddest, ripest apple he'd ever seen. He ran across the trunks where unpruned trees had split and died, lifting his toes above roots that grabbed like hands. He pumped his knees, sprinting toward the apple, fruit of his life, which seemed all the more valuable because it was in his orchard. Benjamin had reached that pitch where every physical movement seemed symbolic. His mouth was dry. He felt a slight chill. He wished Louie could see him run. It seemed he'd been running through this orchard all his life, seeking this sweet, forbidden fruit.

Benjamin reached the tree, panting. Sweat poured in his eyes, and his shirt was slavered to his skin. He shivered in wind from the mountains, heaving and seized by cramps, hardly able to straighten up. The apple dangled inches above his fingers. He did not notice that his throbbing hand was nearly as red as the fruit. He teetered on his toes and reached up.

Amy stopped at the gate. As she watched Benjamin run toward the tree, she saw a knight flying through a gauntlet to capture a golden apple. Then she was crashing behind him, her red hair tearing through branches and glowing in patches of sun. She burst into the clearing and stopped.

The apple jiggled on its stem. Benjamin grasped it and pulled. The bough bent down and the apple broke off. He held it in his palms and gazed up almost shyly. They stared at each other, circled by serpentine branches. Melting frost glistened on the apple's bruised skin. Benjamin felt a mushy spot and smelled a sharp odor. His fingers sank into a pulpy mass eaten out by worms, and rancid juice ran down his wrists. The apple was frozen rotten.

With a pang, he held it out to her, gesturing silently. *Take my apple.*

Amy's nostrils quivered at the sweet, pungent fragrance of the snow apple. So this was why he'd brought her to his garden. To offer a forbidden fruit.

Benjamin held out the decayed apple, a seed sown in the Depression magically brought to fruition.

Taking the apple in her cupped palms, Amy lifted her eyes to his with silent appreciation. Wrinkling her nose, she bit into the rimy skin and spat out the rottenness. The seeds tasted nutty and bittersweet, as befit the giver.

The snow apple melted with a wisp of steam in the sun.

CHAPTER 25

I t began to snow. The flakes melted on Benjamin's face and cooled his blood. They walked back through the bluing streets to the hotel. The room was a box of American emptiness, Benjamin thought, unable to explain the feelings welling up inside him. A framed lithograph of Moses looking down from Mount Nebo to the Promised Land hung crookedly above the twin beds. He took off his snowy hat: his head burned like a Franklin stove, but his wet suit gave him a chill. Benjamin sat on the edge of the bed and began to take off his shoes, but the weight of the ice-crusted soles pulled him down. Pools gathered at his heels. He shook himself and realized he'd drowsed off. Joggers ran for miles and here he was, exhausted after a little hike! At least he'd reached the garden, passed the apple to the next runner. The weight of the world. Amy'd have to carry it best she could. It had been ugly as sin in his hands, but the juice running down her arms was beautiful, he thought, before slipping off again.

Amy took off his wet coat and trousers and levered his feet -- they were almost blue -- onto the bed and pulled down the covers and tucked him in under the sheet. He curled on his side, his cheeks rosy, almost like a child's. She turned out the light and picked up her purse and scarf to go look for food. She would surprise him with a candlelight dinner. She paused at the door and looked back; the ravages of the trip made him look haggard and shrunken -- his flesh sagged beneath the youthful flush.

She began to close the door and Benjamin stirred awake. He peered at her through his fever, feeling the cool imprint of her palm on his forehead like a pond fending off a forest fire. He was too weak to ask where she was going. He only managed to lift his hand as she put her fingers to her lips. The door shut, and for a long time the image of her smile persisted.

Benjamin relaxed in the heat of his body. Fever was old hat to him. Ever since he'd contracted malaria on the river, he'd had an annual recurrence of chills. Winter in North America meant the rainy season in the Amazon, and the little malaria parasites swam upstream in his blood with the doggedness of expatriate Cariocas reenacting Carnival in New York.

He'd confused the symptoms at first with the tropical Garden of Eden, but now he recognized the heat was in his blood. Only it was tricky, like Carnival, because once the little buggers started to dance, you never knew what was real or what was fantasy. That's what he loved about Brazil, you couldn't get it out of your blood: saudade, that untranslatable word of longing, was a physical reaction -- a tugging at the heart, a freezing in the loins -- that melted feelings like snow and ravaged like a fever.

He stood up, feeling lightheaded, navigated across the rising-and-falling floor to the bathroom. It seemed strange to be suffering a tropical fever during a snowstorm, but he had just the thing to bring down his temperature. He rummaged in his Dopp kit and pulled out a green bottle of Novoforma, a Brazilian pain formula. Novoforma was banned by the FDA in America because it brought down 104-degree fever in just minutes and made a sick person feel fit enough to work even though he could lie in bed and collect health insurance. But the manufacturer had no compunction about exporting it to the Third World. The tiny Portuguese print on the label warned it could cause kidney, heart, and or female damage, but Benjamin had been popping them for years. You just sweated a little when the Novoforma flushed out the fever, then you were fine until you needed the next dose: two pills every four hours. Benjamin put four on his tongue, washed them down with tap water, pulled on his tropical pajama bottoms, dragged a towel back to bed, and climbed under the blankets, wondering where Amy had gone so long. His heart pounded, his veins distended, and sweat poured out of his limbs. He closed his eyes and sank past guilt and longing, into the deepest slumber he'd had since returning to America. He felt cool as the snow falling outside the window.

He awoke about 11 p.m. He felt no pain and cracked open his eyes and started. Two white candles burned at the foot of the bed. Amy sat in a straight-backed chair, her hands folded in her lap.

"I've died and gone to heaven?" he swallowed, sitting up in bed.

"The chicken's cold." She pointed peevishly at a wilted bird, trussed with dental floss and garlanded with sprigs of parsley, which she'd bought pre-roasted and tried unsuccessfully to keep warm on the radiator. "I had dinner ready, but I didn't want to wake you. Aren't you hungry?"

Benjamin remembered Louie. "I was just dreaming of Mama's matzo-ball soup."

Amy covered her suitcase with a folded sheet and made a table. She placed the candles on top and put the white grocery bags on their heads as party hats. They ate with plastic forks and shared a bottle of cheap wine. The sweet taste made Benjamin choke. He swallowed and his face darkened.

"I'm sorry I dragged you out there. I didn't mean for you to eat that apple."

"Why?"

"Because you have enough problems. You could get sick."

This struck Amy as strange. First he led her on and now he was backing off.

"Why? Do you have herpes?"

He nearly bit off the wishbone. "What are you talking about?"

"When a man gives a woman an apple in the Garden of Eden, it can only mean one thing."

Benjamin blushed to the back of his head. He drained his glass and poured another. "I meant the Apple of Knowledge," he sputtered. The wine emboldened him. "But thanks for thinking I was a dirty old man."

"Aren't you?"

The picture of Moses seemed to turn away. They both reached for napkins at the same moment. Amy grasped his hand. She pulled him toward her. Benjamin's knee tipped over the suitcase, spilling chicken onto the sheet and knocking the candles onto the floor. The light sputtered out. He landed in her lap. Amy crushed Benjamin to her. She covered his bristly face with kisses. He was feverishly overcome with thirst. He could not get enough of her lips, her eyes, her neck. She fountained up to him, an endless stream, a source he had been searching for everywhere but in Amy. He drank at her breasts, in the depression of her ribs, in her armpits. He could feel her heart beating beneath her ribs, her blood rushing through her veins, her cool body washing him with a replenishing stream that touched him where her arms hugged his back, where her elbows gripped his chest, where her hands rubbed his ears and his throat. Benjamin crushed his lips to her navel. He drank from the cool white pool shimmering in snow light.

Amy was so surprised by the onslaught that she forgot to be afraid. Benjamin's moustache tickled her stomach. She wanted him to undress her. But even as she thought this, Benjamin pulled back.

"I don't know what came over me," he apologized, sitting up.

Amy lay exposed. Her thin wool sweater had been pulled up. Her bra dangled, exposing the depression at her breastbone. A fringe of pubic hair appeared where he had kissed. She turned away.

Benjamin felt dizzy. Was it the fever? Or guilt? He escaped to the bathroom and drank from the tap. He splashed his face and took a handful of Novoforma. He could hear her stifled crying above the water running down the drain.

Finally, Benjamin tiptoed out of the bathroom in his bare feet. He was wearing two bath towels draped over his shoulder and coiled around his waist like a toga. His heart quickened as he approached Amy's snowdrift figure.

She lay on the floor, twisted on her side with her torso facing him and her hips and thighs turned toward the mattress. He stepped on the pickle jar, nearly breaking his foot, and skidded on the chicken grease. Amy pretended not to hear. Her face was half-covered by the sheet. She imagined Benjamin dressed as a Roman, with a fringe of hair haloed out to the sides. His eyes twinkled like a cross-eyed Plato. She worried that he was going to fall -- or launch into a philosophical discourse -- but he caught himself and said nothing. He plunged his arms under her and swept her up. Tottering a bit, he carried her over to the bed. He set her down like a bride on the sheets. He held his toga with one hand and unlaced her shoes. The gentle touches teased Amy. Her body grew warm. Her breathing sped up. But she remained stiff and cold. She could not be turned on and off like a switch.

Benjamin had gotten her undressed and between the sheets when he felt trouble under his toga. Years had passed -- who was counting? -- since he'd last made love. The closest thing to it had been getting aroused in a top-less show in New York after dropping off his manuscript at a publisher. He wasn't sure his equipment worked.

"One second--" He leaped up and rummaged in his suitcase. In case his book was accepted, he'd brought a can of oysters from New York to celebrate.

"What are you doing?" Amy asked.

"It's an old Brazilian custom--" He downed the entire tin of oysters, ascribed to have magical potency.

For good measure he did ten deep-knee bends to get his blood circulating.

"Come back," she sighed at his shenanigans.

All Benjamin needed to hear was her asking him. Stealing back through the dark, he felt the attraction of youth and age drawn together against life's limits. He felt like the sexiest thing in the world.

He took off his toga in the dark. She felt warm and silky.

Their bodies fit together. His hot forehead touched her cool cheek. His large nose pressed against her ear. His moustache tickled her nose. His burning eyes were open, Amy's closed. His barrel chest filled the depression between her breasts. His curved spine took the weight from her concave hips. His thin legs rested lightly on her fleshy thighs. Her knees raised and opened. His knees dug into the mattress.

They clung to one another, but when Amy felt him stiffening, she froze.

"Benjamin, I don't have any protection--" She pushed him away.

"I thought every woman in your generation was on the pill."

"They're bad for your health."

"So is life!" He was accustomed to another birth control method, primitive but functional.

Benjamin pulled on his trousers, stuffed his bare feet into his shoes, grabbed his jacket, and took the elevator down to the lobby. With his blood pumping Novoforma, he felt tropically warm.

The night clerk gave a withering look to the apoplectic codger who flopped sockless toward him, with his hair puffed out and a jacket pulled over his bare chest.

The clerk was sure the TV had broken down and this pensioner had nothing better to do than ask him to fix it at 2 a.m., even though the Moab station had stopped broadcasting an hour ago. He was used to complaints and assumed an unruffled demeanor to show his disdain and readied a copy of *TV Guide* to prove his point.

"Do you have any prophylactics?" Benjamin panted, holding up his pants under his coat like Napoleon.

The clerk stifled a laugh. "You? What do you need them for -- water balloons?"

"What do you mean, what do I need them for?" Benjamin roared.

The clerk looked him up and down. Benjamin drew himself up, displaying his chest, carpeted with white hair.

"How many you want?" the clerk asked. "They're $2.50 a shot."

"Two."

"Two?" he smirked.

"Four -- unlubricated!" Benjamin buttoned his coat. "The night is young."

Amy was holding the sheets up to her neck when he returned with the brown paper bag. She looked small and uncertain. But the sight of Benjamin stomping in, cursing the clerk, made her open the sheets. His body was cold. His breath smelled of oysters. He edged toward the bathroom and opened a bottle of mouthwash.

"Don't. You smell like the sea."

"You know why I wrote *Pearls?*" he asked, climbing in beside her. "To remember to bring oysters tonight. You know why I bought that orchard forty years ago? To give you the apple today."

"That's what you tell all the women," she chided him. But she wanted to believe they were meant to be here tonight, that it wasn't accident that had brought them to this bed in Moab.

"If I hadn't been raped, I wouldn't be here," she confessed. But she didn't soften her words, because that was the reason she was with him now, to face her fear with an older, gentler man. His penis brushed her and she was pierced by the depth of her feeling for Benjamin. He rolled onto her. Unconsciously, she tensed her thighs, feeling a wave of fear coming over her.

"Open up," he whispered.

Amy lay beneath him, terrified of the vulnerability of giving herself to a man.

But he kissed her and she opened and Benjamin penetrated her and she felt she was opening herself to life, to all the possibilities of creation.

This is my pearl, Benjamin thought, rocking in and out of her hips, smelling the scent of perlas from the Amazon in her breasts. This is what I sought, calling it a million other names, he thought, exercising that great personal capacity that Benjamin East possessed -- to believe.

He raised himself on his hands and gazed at the yellowed lithograph of the prophet looking plaintively over the Promised Land he would never reach. He looked at the milk and honey of Amy's body rolling beneath him. The most impossible dream was the one that came true.

"Eat your heart out Moses!" his soul crowed.

They sweated and rocked and rose. A million sensations swarmed through Benjamin's body. Amy looked imperious above him, her red hair tossing like a lion's mane. Her breasts shone with perspiration. Her nipples jigged as her ribs pressed against her flesh and then disappeared in the circular motions of her hips, vast as the constellations. She seemed lost in another world, squatting on top of him. A world where she was not afraid to display the primitivity that made her draw up her knees and squat on her heels and squeeze him. This was the naked, uninhibited Amy that had been hidden across the states. Her eyes flashed and her teeth shone as her throat reverberated with grunts. The inside of her mouth was raw. In the silvery snow light, her movements were as unintelligible as the revolutions of the stars. She was free, liberated from the limits she had known even a month ago, lost in the salty smell of oysters and the heady, tropical scent of his cologne. She would not go back.

Benjamin shut his eyes and watched currents of color well up and swirl beneath his eyelids, painting the gyrating motions of her body in pastel rainbows across his fevered mind. She had turned his abandoned orchard into a blooming garden!

His flesh hung flaccidly from his bones and he was not flexible like a young man, but she could feel his sturdy frame working like a locomotive. Most of all she imagined Benjamin was a buffalo. His huge back covered with wooly hair, his thin arms and legs planted like hooves, his round eyes huge and unblinking. She fantasized he was the last member of a nearly extinct species of blue-eyed buffalo, a thundering fast-talker, an idealistic survivor of another age, who charged into her life and showed her the world unfenced.

They slowed down, their legs and knees tangled as they shifted and Benjamin was above her, his torso propped up on his hoof-like hands, his heavy head hanging beneath his shoulders. They had been making love for at least a hundred years, Benjamin thought, unblinking, but still he reveled that the moment had not ended. He felt the unity he imagined was the state of the oyster's peace. How myriad were the possibilities to be a grain of sand, a banana leaf, a mountain stream, he thought as Amy stopped humming and reached that point of ecstasy when her body became clay in his hands, infinitely changeable and cohesive.

He convulsed. Amy trembled, sweaty and acrid and satisfied. Benjamin felt faint. He approached that ultimate frontier where anything seemed possible and reached one step further, "Amy." The blood rushed from Benjamin's head and he blanked out.

Then the blood came back, bringing with it chills. He throbbed from his prostate to his fingertips as he kneeled, wrung out and exhausted, feeling the unexpected rise of nausea and shooting pains. He felt as terrible as he had felt wonderful. He didn't want to disturb Amy with it. He only needed to sleep. He sank into the soft sheets and breathed thinly as the fever overcame him, sweeping him into unconsciousness.

Amy tucked Benjamin under the blanket and let him sleep. She kissed his damp forehead and propped herself up beside him on her elbow. She felt physically and spiritually cleansed. Outside the snow had blanketed the parking lot. It looked like a clean slate.

CHAPTER 26

A t dawn, Benjamin rocked deliriously between the mattress and the wall. His right shoulder throbbed and his left hand was numb. He burrowed in the crack, trying to crawl out of the dugout. His hot breath rasped from papery lips. He moaned in fits. His eyes glittered like coals in the paper lantern of his skull.

"Gisela, I'll get help," he rambled in Portuguese, hallucinating he was in the Amazon.

His anguished rocking awakened Amy. Her first thought was that he was having a nightmare.

"Benjamin, wake up!" She hugged his burning body to her breast. He didn't answer. He stared right at her -- his eyes looked like they were going to burn out.

"Gisela, me perdoe." *Forgive me.*

Amy panicked. She ran to the bathroom for water and found his pills spilled all over the sink. She ran back, propped him up, forced a few drops between his cracked lips, splashed the rest on his face, and swabbed off his chest with a sopping towel. He seemed to revive and recognize her.

"You all right?" he asked, patting her hand. Then his expression changed and he reached out, as if to comfort her. "Gisela, don't cry, we can try again."

"Benjamin, what are these?" Amy almost screamed, holding the round white pills. They shone luminously like the shells the delegado had given him. And her skin was fragrant.

"Perolas?" he smiled.

"How many did you take?" she shouted.

But Benjamin didn't hear for the rushing of water, reaching from the canoe for the shimmering whites of Gisela's eyes reflected in the river. He reached and nearly touched her and the canoe rolled over and he splashed into the water, breaking her face into a thousand fragments, and she sank like a stone to the bottom, clawing mud and sand. He couldn't breathe. Tears choked his throat. He had never let himself cry after her death; never broken down, and now it didn't matter. He embraced the darkness, demanding nothing, receiving all that had ever slipped through his fingers. He approached an unfathomable state of peace and then felt a rope pulling, twisting, and jerking him back.

Amy had dragged him out of bed, across the carpet, over the bathtub's lion paws, and dropped him clanging into the tub. She twisted on the cold tap and, before he could drown, ran out half-naked into the hall and got a scoop of ice from the ice machine and threw it in the water.

Benjamin writhed in searing agony.

Amy boiled water on the hot plate and brewed tea. As the ice cubes bobbed in the water, she forced the boiling brew down his throat. She was plunged in torment, but her body moved with supple energy, as if the sap squeezed out of his body had made hers bloom. His skin, white as the porcelain tub, turned red and blue from the cracking ice and steam, the most beautiful colors in the world.

Benjamin opened his eyes and thought he was going over Iguacu falls in a dugout.

"I'm going to crack!" he yelled. "Hand me my medicine."

"I will not," she hollered back, forcing tea down his throat. "You gave me a scare."

"It's just a touch of spring fever. Be reasonable," he pleaded, peering over the tub. Her pale breasts were like the honeysuckle flowers he crushed to his nose when he last stood on the balcony before leaving Rio. He couldn't be mad at her for tearing out his heart, but he couldn't stand to look at her any longer either. "All right, then go out and get me some aspirin and quinine tonic." He banged the tub for emphasis, it sounded more like a weak bell than a gong, but Amy acquiesced and ran out.

It was after dawn, the light almost day-glow orange on the icy streets, and she sprinted in the cold wind, feeling guilty for his sickness, but fresh and supple.

The general practitioner in a rumpled suit and cowboy boots brought a brusque Western bedside manner into the room. He looked into Benjamin's dilated eyes, thumped his chest, listened to his heart with a cold stethoscope, read off his temperature on a fancy digital thermometer, and asked Amy what had brought on the fever.

"Intercourse," she answered.

He didn't bat an eye, although he smiled at the suffering patient. After learning a few more details, he listened to Benjamin's heart again, but the beat was strong and regular.

Benjamin awakened to the cold metal ring of the stethoscope on his back and immediately started abusing the doctor. He jabbed at the quack with a forefinger, telling him he couldn't distinguish the symptoms of malaria from Rocky Mountain fever. He was having a mild recurrence of an old ailment and had taken a couple of Brazilian aspirin, that was all, he insisted.

He fooled no one, but his orneriness heartened Amy. Dr. Clayton took blood and urine samples, gave Benjamin a shot of penicillin, prescribed aspirin, fluids, and bed rest. He said Benjamin could stay in the hotel.

"And no more sex for a week!" he made Benjamin promise, winking at the patient from the door. In the hall, he told Amy he doubted it was malaria. "Not after twenty-five years. It could be a virus, or exhaustion," he speculated, trying to offer a hint of what she was dealing with. "Or it could be something else."

"Like what?" she asked, whitening.

"I could put him in the hospital and give him a dozen tests, and we'd begin to find out. But basically if you ran the tests you'd find out he's a seventy-year-old geriatric."

"He's sixty-eight, not seventy! I'll take care of him here," she shouted to her own surprise.

Doc Clayton smiled ruefully, lines creasing his cheeks. "I think that's fine, if you're willing to do it. I was going to say that people do better when they're nursed at home. I don't know your relationship, but after he gets better, if you want to continue with him to California, I'd say go ahead and let him get checked out by a doctor out there. He's isolated here and it's better to be at home, with his own people."

He left and Amy turned back to the door. A part of her wanted to run back and tell the doctor Benjamin had no people, no home. But she opened the door and went to the colorless man lying asleep in the bed. Last night he had opened her to love on this same bed. She couldn't help it, she just kept opening.

The next few days she endured the bedpan side of caring for him by forcing herself to sketch when he slept. The stench and ugliness did not stop her from being tender, but she was not interested in self-sacrifice. She sat in the old wooden chair and drew pastels of the hotel room, portrait sketches of Benjamin, a Japanese perspective looking down at the snowy parking lot. She didn't feel trapped; she'd opened up to accept responsibility in her freedom. She did not think about the future. She didn't dwell on what had happened. She nursed Benjamin and filled her sketchbook with pictures.

It was her first vaguely mature work. Her lines were deft; the figures were more sensitively evoked than any of her drawings of New York, as if what Benjamin had taught her about touching life and not pulling back had penetrated her hands. In a strange way, she understood what the professor at Cooper Union had meant when he'd told her to go live with her husband and paint her family, her home. At this moment Benjamin was her family, this room her home. In cobalt blue and vermillion, she shaded the room. Flowing lines had replaced the stiffness of her earlier drawings. The figures were infused with Benjamin's dash of the impossible, through vibrant contrasts of color.

Benjamin's face was blue in one picture; his hands clutched a green sheet at his chin. Her own self-portrait in the mirror was yellow, but her thin lips and wide eyes stared out clearly.

To open up yet not lose herself; this was the seed Benjamin had planted in her even as the condom was flushed down the toilet.

One evening -- the dawns and dusks seemed to run together - Benjamin groaned and tossed. He appeared to be muttering in a delirium of pain, but he was crooning snatches of an Al Jolson song:

There's a rainbow 'round my shoulder
And a sky of blue above
I'm shoutin' so
The world will know, that
I'm in love!

He felt indefinable joy. He felt oceanic. He gave up trying to analyze it. He was tired of words. The music seemed to say it better. He could barely move, but his mind stretched to pluck out memories with infinite reach.

He remembered once when the rains of March flooded Rio, he awoke at night with the rain banging on the tin roof. The bed was empty. He found Gisela standing naked on her tiptoes in the garden, drenched like some primeval goddess. His eyes opened. Amy sat drawing by the window.

On the third evening, he felt a glow of recovery and climbed out of bed. He looked in the mirror with shock and saw a shrunken man with neck cords, deep lines in his face, and wild hair. The fever had made it grow. At first he hardly recognized himself, you old Don Juan. He walked around in his pajamas, which hung loose on his gaunt frame, sporting the aura of a survivor.

The next morning, when Amy first saw him dressed in his Brazilian suit, huge and slack on his shoulders, brushing his few wisps of hair and preening with a concave smile, she stopped back her tears and ran outside. In the distance, she could barely make out the brown blur of the withered orchard. This is what the apple of love did to Benjamin. She cursed life.

Benjamin took the opportunity of her absence to place a long-distance call. "Hello, Lou?" he shouted, flushing with excitement, when he heard his brother's growl. Then weakness from the chills brought Benjamin's shout down to a croak.

"Terrible," he answered, when Lou asked about his health.

"What's wrong?" cried Lou, frightened.

"Chest pains worse than yours."

He wanted to make Lou comfortable. To impress him with his credentials in the bad health department. "I got nausea, shooting pains you wouldn't believe. Diarrhea! What? I don't hear so well either," he threw in for the hell of it. "No, I'm not in the hospital," he answered Lou's question, affronted. "Oh, and my enlarged prostate!" He finished his list with pride. He was unable to stop himself from hinting about his sexual adventure. "Lou, I just wanted to hear your voice."

"My voice?" Lou asked, trying to piece together what his brother was up to by this phony display of ill health and nostalgia. He concluded that the list of complaints would wind up with a plea for money. "So, you're broke!" he cackled. "How much do you need -- a grand?"

"Your company," whispered Benjamin. "I want to have some arguments. Maybe even some peace." He swallowed hard. How strange his thoughts in words. "No, I'm not on drugs! I'm trying to tell you I want to be with you. These twenty-five year-old women are too much for me. No more sex orgies."

"Orgies!" Louie whooped. "Ben, what do you mean?"

"Just once," Benjamin coughed. "It was wonderful."

Louie's cigar fell out of his mouth. "With that waif?"

"Yeah, the apple of my life," Benjamin admitted. But the conversation enervated him. "Look, let's be realistic, Lou. I don't want to hurt her feelings. Making whoopie was nice, but I can't do it again. I haven't told her yet." And for a minute, Benjamin couldn't speak, for he hadn't yet told this to himself. A shooting pain stabbed his arm. Was he trying to hold onto her? "Lou, life's too short. I'm trying to be realistic, no more goose chases. I've learned my lesson from *Pearls*. I'm not a writer. There's so much beyond words. Like being together. You're alive. I'm still kicking... The doctor says I can go to California. I promised to take Amy to San Francisco, but that's the end of it." He didn't want that for a minute, but he knew it was inevitable. Love can't stand still. He had to prepare himself to separate now, or force her to do it and lose his self-respect and a chance to remain friends. "Then, either I find a place for the East brothers out there, or I come home to New York -- not Long Island." The phone hung silent in his hand. He wanted to tell Lou he loved him, but he saved that for next time. "Either way, we'll be together."

"Yeah, together." Lou actually sounded touched. "I'm glad you called. I'll think about it."

Benjamin hung up, relieved but drained. Amy's seat by the window was empty. It struck him for the first time -- the trip was ending. It hurt more than any physical pain, but he packed his bag.

The next afternoon they left Moab. Benjamin insisted on climbing aboard the bus without assistance. Amy smiled as he whistled, "California, here I come."

The orchard disappeared in the rear window and they melted into the stream of travelers, boarding and off-loading in a blur of local bus stops that resembled each other, among a flux of people who looked alike, through a system that treated humans like baggage, across a desert that was of interest to nobody. But they were insulated by the bus, comforted by the ritual of travel.

They passed Salt Lake City in darkness. As they skirted the black lake ringed by luminous salt, Benjamin did what he'd been fighting not to do since they left Moab.

"I'm going to be busy when we get to San Francisco," he hinted. "I'll be hunting for an apartment, renewing my passport, signing up for golden-age benefits, playing the tax loopholes. You'll have to fend for yourself."

"Why can't we stay together?"

"For how long? A week, a month? Until you meet a friend and bring him home and there's this man old enough to be your father waiting in the living room? Hell no! I wouldn't want to be put in that position and I wouldn't want you to be jealous if I met some eligible widow." The thought made his stomach turn, but he had thought this speech through and he wanted to deliver it before he chickened out. "I want to thank you for helping me. You were a terrific nurse."

"Benjamin, why are you saying this?"

"Because it needs to be said. You were a terrific nurse, but you're not a nurse. You've got your whole life ahead of you and I don't want you to begin it with distractions. I can take care of myself."

They crossed the Great Salt Desert, passing the state line into Nevada near midnight. The sky was clear and the moon hung over the Independence Mountains as they passed the lights of Wells, following the bed of the Humboldt River to Elko and up the 6,114-foot Emigrant Pass. Benjamin could see desert and mountains reaching all the way to California. He'd awaited this last leg of the trip so expectantly. Now he wanted it to last a little longer. The very names of the land formations played tricks on him, parodying his relationship with Amy. Independence! Emigrant Pass! Battle Mountain! Lovelock! He could not have written his feelings better than the signposts by the road.

Near daybreak, they reached Reno. They had an hour layover between buses. Amy found Benjamin a bench and excused herself. His courage in telling her he was going to be on his own made her want to sever her own ties -- not to him -- but to the past. She looked at her ring finger, a stripe of pale skin where the wedding band had blocked the sun. She'd taken it off a month before, but she was still legally married to Ray. Before she reached California, she had to do something about it.

Benjamin squinted as Amy walked away under a pink neon sign advertising: "24-hour Wedding Chapel." Where was she going? Anything was possible, and his will started caving in immediately with fantasies of marriage. Stranger things have happened in Reno, he mused, thinking of septuagenarian movie producers who wedded their starlets. And he and Amy had proved themselves in bed! He lounged in the seat, projecting Tahoe wedding scenes on the terrazzo floor.

Amy turned back from the door: Benjamin looked so devilishly angelic on the chair, his blue eyes grown huge in his shrunken face, his wispy hair glowing. He looked up, and they both smiled, wondering what the other one was thinking. Benjamin groped in his pocket for a ring. He found the crumpled cigar Louie had given him, slipped off the cellophane wrapper, and pulled off the red and gold band. But Amy only saw a wizened man with a confused look in his eye, and the shadow of senility flew over.

She turned away and hurried to the phone. Benjamin put the cigar down on the bench and handed the ring to a round-eyed four-year-old boy who was pestering his mother.

"Look at that -- a secret signet ring," Benjamin winked, patting the child's head, feeling strength in the boy's curly hair.

Amy stopped before a law office offering "Reno Discount Divorces." With a determined look, she crossed the street to a pay phone, scrounged a quantity of dimes from her purse, and dialed Ray. She braced herself against the phone booth and heard the buzzer in Ray's office. She'd forgotten that sound, a buzz not a ring, and it brought back all her fears, as if only a moment ago he'd pinned her down and -- "Hullo..." Ray's voice sounded strangely soft and drawling, bringing back a golden day when they'd lain down on the bank of the Shenandoah in the dappled shadow of a dogwood. Amy had forgotten that side of Ray, too. Forgotten the Southern gentleness of Virginia.

"Ray," she stammered, torn between the two pictures. "I'm in Reno. I wanted--" But what did she want? She winced, digging her fingernails into the scarred wood and twisting the steel-wrapped cord.

Ray broke in, "Honey, I've been searching all over for you. Oh Jesus, you called! Are you all right? Forgive what I done."

She wanted to be big enough not to hate him, to let it pass. But she found herself shouting, "I can't. I can't forgive you, Ray."

"You don't have to. I just want you to come back," Ray said. "Now that you've had your fling, don't forget you're my wife. Don't do anything funny out there in Reno."

The blood was nearly gone from her hand, but she tightened her grip on the cord and pressed her head against the scratched wood. "Ray, I'm sorry for keeping you in the dark all these weeks. But I had to leave, had to get far away. Now I've decided. I'm not coming back." The finality of her decision didn't surprise her. "It's over. I want a divorce."

Benjamin was asleep again -- he seemed to relax and doze more easily now -- when Amy came back with a cup of coffee and a cigarette after her call. She had never smoked in her life, but now she needed a cigarette. The bus was boarding and she touched Benjamin's shoulder and he stirred and opened his eyes, almost like a child. For a moment, he looked up at the 24-hour marriage chapel sign, wondering if she was now a free woman. But Amy spied where he was looking. "Come on, we'll miss the bus."

They sat down in the middle section of the San Francisco Express, adjusted their recliners, and pretended everything was normal, that this ride was no different than the others. The bus climbed out of the desert into mountains. Cold mists clung to the rocky slopes. Rain streaked the windows. The fifteen or so passengers sat in cavernous silence. Donner Pass was socked in, and Benjamin felt lost in the clouds.

The bus zigzagged down switchbacks, and he smiled. Then Amy clenched his fingers and he realized she was feeling the same dread of the last stop. The switchbacks lengthened into straight inclines. He was holding onto her, he knew. But he'd get over that. He wanted to help her start off on the right foot, not waste even a day. Amy might be all right in the travel department, but he hadn't taught her a thing about making it in the real world. He looked at her sleepy eyes. She reminded him of his younger self, arriving in Brazil with a wool suit and a can of Maxwell House coffee. If he let her go now, she'd make as big a mess of herself as he had.

The bus gathered speed. They plunged through evergreens wreathed in mist, losing altitude until the seasons seemed to change. Before them, the Sacramento Valley spread its lush green fields. Benjamin sniffed the heavy scent of citrus groves, the sweet odor of melons fattened on the vine, the heady damask of vineyards. California ain't no Garden of Eden; it's the kingdom of agribusiness, he admitted with a sigh. His chin jutted with envy at what he could have done with such land. But he took off his hat to the competition.

"It looks like they planted the fields with a computer," Amy said, intimidated by industrialized farms so much larger than anything she'd ever seen in the Shenandoah Valley.

"Face the future!" Benjamin thundered. "In Moab you can eat rotten apples, but here they invented the Apple computer!" Her eyes looked wounded, uncomprehend-ing. He didn't know if he could follow his own advice, but he knew Amy had to confront the microchip on which the circuitry of the new world was printed.

"I just want to be an artist," she said.

"California is the state of the art!" He closed his eyes and conjured up the transcendental frontier according to Benjamin East. "Artists are pioneers who venture into the future and make it in their own image."

"What's that supposed to mean?" she yelled.

"It means you step off the boat and grab the first op-portunity in sight. Even if it hurts. When my father landed at Ellis Island, a nice little tomato vendor offered to watch his luggage while he looked for a rooming house. When Pop came back, the trunk was gone -- eve-ry thread he owned. But the thief's tomatoes were lying there. Tomatoes were poison in the old country. But my father had nothing else, so he ate one and he didn't die, so he started hawking them on the dock. And other peo-ple bought them. Opportunity wasn't poison in America. And that's how the tailor became a green grocer, how we survived--"

He grabbed her wrist and pointed at the suburbs or-biting beside the freeway. "I don't know California from the moon, but I bet it can still be done. We're going to blow into San Francisco and get jobs the first day!"

"Why the first day?"

"Because," he sputtered, "because we can't afford to lose time." He released her wrist. "Shake?"

Amy cringed at his desperation, but she understood his fear and she shook. Benjamin wasn't finished. His chin jutted as he clutched her hand.

"Then we're on our own."

CHAPTER 27

B enjamin and Amy pulled into the San Francisco
depot at eleven in the morning, just when the fog
was burning off the pavement. "Goodbye dog,"
Benjamin whispered, patting the fender. He held Amy's
hand as she climbed off. The seedy terminal, surrounded
by leprous flophouses and derelict bars, was not an aus-
picious place to start a new life. But to Amy the collection of aging hippies, despondent Chicano families, 9th
Street winos, cultist flower sellers, and peacock cowboys
seemed to glow with a San Francisco aura. People
sprawled on the floor and lounged on the pavement,
which impressed her with the West Coast's looseness,
and the crushed velvet costumery gave a feeling of at-
tempts at creativity. She was in too much of a hurry to
linger.

Benjamin bought a copy of the *San Francisco Chronicle*.
It was Tuesday, January 20, 1981. Back in Washington,
D.C., Governor Ronald Reagan was being sworn in as

President. There were unconfirmed reports that the American hostages were being released from Iran.

"A new era!" he rejoiced, or pretended to for Amy's sake. She'd stormed into his life a day after he'd landed in Miami, on the 9th of December 1980. That Day of Infamy, when Customs seized Zazza, was 42 days ago. Poor Zazza, had she died in captivity? So much had happened on the road trip, now it was ending, and a new stage was beginning. Benjamin felt the brim of his cap to make sure her bright orange flight feather was still there.

Amy nudged his elbow and he looked up. Businesses would be closed in six hours; the thing was to start looking immediately. "Where's a safe place for our stuff?" she asked, remembering the story about the immigrants' luggage being stolen at Ellis Island.

Benjamin grinned down to his neck cords, relishing Amy's anxiousness -- a little bit of caution was good for her. They found a bank of 24-hour coin lockers, stowed their bags, and took the numbered keys.

Unburdened, Amy's arms felt like wings. She wore a brown corduroy suit with a matching vest, and her hair, drawn back, revealed the outline of her face: under the clouded eyebrows, clear eyes; her nose, though small, had character after all, and her lips weren't set in a pout. She was not yet beautiful, but no longer cute. Benjamin wore his blue Broadway suit, which hung loose, but crisp -- Amy had pressed it in Moab -- and sported his flowered Brazilian necktie, for good luck. His coloring was pink, his pupils were sharp, and his step light and agile. The last stage had tired him, but when he stepped onto San Francisco pavement, his knees bent and his shoulders tensed as if ready for an earthquake, or excited for one, Amy couldn't tell.

Benjamin sat her down at a coffee counter and opened up the want ads.

"Welcome to the real world." He spread the morning paper before her. Amy scanned the front page. "Economic indicators down, inflation rising." *The Chronicle* had played this recession story whenever there wasn't a local mass murder to sell papers, for years. San Francisco had one of the highest unemployment rates, new folks kept pouring in, attracted by the cable cars, the gay community, and the Hippie image, faster than the economy could absorb them.

Benjamin watched her face fall. That was America. They put the bad news on the front page and sandwich the opportunities inside. But he didn't say anything. He had a vastly more important quest. To taste a California orange.

He left her marking up the want ads and went prowling the streets for a Farmer's Market. The fog had lifted and the air was blue and crisp on 8th Street; he wandered between old standup lunch bars, skirted a block-long hole in the ground where an urban renewal project was going up, and reached a highway underpass. The market had been torn down, but he saw a man selling a pyramid of oranges from a pickup truck.

"Beautiful, big as a grapefruit." Benjamin wished Louie could see it.

"Then you ain't seen much." The orange vendor spoke with an Okie twang. He was a tall scarecrow of a man in his sixties with grey sideburns. "But they're a sight better than them malathion-tainted buggers they sell up at the supermarket!"

"Been here long?" Benjamin asked, glancing at his watch.

"Oh, about fifteen years. My pa used to truck greens into the market." The vendor launched into his story. The small truck farms had died and the farmers market had been rooted up. When the market was in its heyday, it was a sight, he crooned. His pa came out from Oklahoma in 1933, and they began as migrant pickers and then bought the first truck... The words rolled on and Benjamin listened. The Depression, the war, the boom, ran through this man's life as through Benjamin's. He felt comforted. He shook the vendor's hand and walked away with two oranges, realizing he'd forgotten to tell the fellow he was the Big Apple. He didn't need to.

When he returned, Amy had covered the want ads with markings, made some half-hearted calls, and come up with an opening -- night guard at the Palace of the Legion of Honor.

"A war memorial?" he asked.

238 • JONATHAN FREEDMAN

"It's also an art museum!" She was excited and in a hurry. "You rest here. I'll be back--"

"Rest?" Benjamin had sat down for a few winks, almost dropping the oranges. He'd only needed a minute to recharge.

Amy smiled. Their relationship had become like a dance. She could predict his steps before he took them.

He squired Amy up Market Street and hailed a cab. They left the Tenderloin and swept beneath the glass-skinned towers of the financial district, past hillside neighborhoods scrawled like Chinese characters, flashing views of cable cars and bay, and they silently savored the unvarnished beauty of the San Francisco of the tourist posters. Then the glamour vanished and it was a cross-town ride through treeless neighborhoods to the imposing Palace of the Legion of Honor on the Palisades overlooking the Golden Gate. With a chill, they entered the fog zone.

Amy nibbled an orange and peered out the window, concentrating on the job interview. Benjamin noticed how absorbed she was. This sudden seizure of practicality pleased him, but the faces and window box flowers and faint smell of the sea aroused his senses. The orange burst open, and its juice ran down his wrists, and the wind riffled the feather in his hat.

Amy imagined the guard job -- having the paintings all to herself in the long hours of the night, then walking home in the misty mornings, catching a few hours' sleep, and painting in the afternoons. She would teach herself directly from the Old Masters, find a studio with a skylight. The skylight was very important in her mind as the fog enshrouded the taxi in the dismal avenues. They turned into a park and she felt like she was entering an impressionist painting. A foghorn blew and the museum drew up, looking like a mausoleum. They paid the taxi and Amy left Benjamin by a stand of wispy pines overlooking the mouth of San Francisco Bay. He waved and she smiled, feeling his support, and disappeared into the museum.

Benjamin walked to the end of the park and sat down on a bench facing the fog-shrouded Golden Gate Bridge. Amy's turmoil scattered to the four winds. He saw a squirrel carry a nut up a tree and disappear in a hole, storing up for the winter. Pigeons settled around the bench pecking for crumbs. He rummaged in his pockets for something to feed them. A few matzo crumbs and the Greyhound ticket was all he had. "You'll have to root for yourselves," he whispered, thinking of Amy and himself. His personal migration was over, but he still needed a nest.

He wanted a place by the water. He'd find something special, maybe across the bridge in Sausalito. He'd heard they had houseboats there, and sunshine, and he'd buy one of those hibachis and cook shrimp on the poop deck and invite Amy to dinner when she needed to get away from the fog. To talk. To draw. Perhaps he'd fix up a spare bunk for her. A place where she could always visit. And then if Louie came to live with him, he'd have to build a two-story houseboat. He dozed before the Golden Gate Bridge, amidst the cooing of pigeons and the crack of clubs against golf balls on the nearby course.

The museum was crowded. Amy took her place at the end of the line and counted thirteen people before her. On the way in, she'd passed a guard. He'd looked like a caged animal. The job was for the day shift, not the night, she found out from the next guy in line. It entailed standing around in a grey uniform and preventing screaming school ninnies from mauling the exhibits. They stood in a tunnel area outside the security chief's office, as one by one they were admitted for an interview. There was a joking camaraderie among the competitors, but underneath it, she felt a terrible desperation emanating from the men who'd been waiting all night to be first in line. They weren't artists. They looked like laid-off construction workers. And she thought what an incredible waste for able-bodied men to have to seek this kind of work. With a little humor, it wouldn't be so bad. Their eyes twinkled with sad hope.

Amy felt the cold of the recession creep into her being. It was not as if only the economy was in a slump -- it was as if vitality had drained from people's blood. She didn't need just a job, she needed a way of defending herself from the recession of the spirit.

She escaped from the line into the cool sunshine -- it was already one o'clock -- and found Benjamin trying to feed a squirrel an orange peel. She touched his shoulder. "I don't want to guard an art mausoleum," she said. "Let's go."

Benjamin nodded, disappointed. A foghorn blew, alarming him. He should reward her for not taking second best! He pulled her down the street to the avenue. They caught a bus back to Market Street, had to stand up the whole way. Amy got a roll of dimes, holed up in a pay phone booth, and called at least twenty listings. She started with Advertising Artist and ended up with Waitress. She put herself in each job, imagining what it would be like. But nobody wanted a wannabe artist without a college degree or relevant experience.

"Come on, I've got an idea." Benjamin comforted her. He didn't have the faintest. But he seized her hand and dragged her out of the booth and up a hill so steep that shallow steps were carved into the cement sidewalk.

"Slow down!" she shouted.

But he was enjoying himself now. No wonder he'd kept falling asleep, his circulation wasn't being used. He'd just read an article about a 68-year-old dentist who'd jogged from California to Washington D.C. A cable car lurched into view. Benjamin sprinted and pulled Amy aboard.

Amy felt released from the desperation of the phone booth. The want ads fluttered away. The city plummeted beneath them.

Panting, holding onto the strap, Benjamin felt like he was swinging on a trapeze. Vistas tipped and sprawled. He blinked for a moment and thought he was riding up Corcovado Mountain, the wooden Bonde train bumping between palm trees and sprays of pink flowers Gisela called Maria Sem Vergonha, *Shameless Mary*, because they bloom anywhere. And they did. But he was gazing at the oriental flower pattern on the dress of a little Chinese girl who sat beside him. And when she saw him smile, she pointed at his moustache, and he twisted up his lips and she laughed, and he glimpsed through the tunnel of years how the world looked to a child -- a dipping, bristling face that smiled when you pointed. He squeezed her cheek and made a sound like he was winding a clock, and she hid her face and peeked out. And, to him, this was the mystery of time that disguised the child's face in the old man's smile.

He was supposed to be helping Amy find a job, but he was absorbed in each moment. The orange, the child, the pigeons. How he missed Zazza! Was she dead or alive? He'd call Customs tomorrow, give the so-and-sos a piece of his mind, ha! Ire roused his spirits.

His thoughts returned to Amy. He could no more wrestle her from her single-minded pursuit than he could communicate his sense of freedom. But his thoughts seemed to draw opportunities toward them. They crested the hill and passed a Chinese man selling tourist paintings of San Francisco. To Benjamin's eyes, the cheesy canvases looked like Michelangelos.

"Look at that art! Go talk to the painter. Maybe you can make a deal to sell your drawings!" He tugged her off the trolley.

Amy winced at the trite pictures of cable cars and looked at the elderly Chinese painter, his face carved like an ivory mask but the eyes twinkling. It was a fallacy to judge a man by his art; the superficiality was deceiving, as in *Pearls*. But that didn't make it art.

"No, let me decide what's good for me," she whispered, dragging Benjamin down the sidewalk.

He stiffened, chastened. Next to the painter stood a man with a shaved head who was selling a tract, "The Riddle of the Universe." The streets of San Francisco were paved with healers, gurus, and mystics proselytizing their philosophies. Benjamin had been drawn to California by a similar impulse, to untangle the riddle of failure, but on the road he'd become disenchanted with his message and enchanted by life. He didn't have the answers -- he shrugged, it now seemed so simple -- no one did. He was glad he didn't feel compelled to stand on a corner and proselytize.

"Let's go up Russian Hill to Coit Tower," Benjamin suggested, squeezing her hand. "I want to show you the bay, not the cheap copies!"

They hiked slowly, pulling themselves up the hill and resting against signposts to catch their breath. Above rose Coit Tower, a Depression-era ziggurat dwarfed by the Transamerica Pyramid stabbing the sky. It was nearly three, and it seemed crazy to waste time detouring to a tourist spot, but when Amy saw the bay sweeping between the bridges, she knew why she'd come to San Francisco.

Benjamin insisted on climbing to the top of the tower. The walls of the spiral staircase were covered with murals painted by WPA artists. The figures were dressed in square-cut, loose-fitting clothes like Benjamin's.

He climbed beside the bushels of apples in the harvest scene, and Amy followed, feeling herself being borne into Benjamin's past. He belonged in the mural, the entrepreneur at the other end of the line, who sold the apples on the street corners of New York. She was inspired to paint her own picture: stiff Depression-realism figures coming off the wall, climbing the stairs, turning into people behind Benjamin -- a living embodiment of their era. A man. Not an ideal. She wanted to tell Benjamin her idea for a portrait, but she would wait until she had a studio.

Benjamin paused on the stairs to catch his breath but heard Amy's footsteps ringing behind him and kept climbing. A force drove him from the murals at the bottom of the tower to the glow of sky at the top. He was testing himself by scaling vertical hills and assaulting stairs. He had always been irrepressible on his first day in a new town. Had to see it from the top! Giddy, he pushed against the wall and mounted the final stair. The Golden Gate Bridge met his eyes. Sweat streamed down his brow and he thought for a moment he was looking down at Rio. San Francisco Bay was the same reef blue as the Bahia de Guanabara, and where Berkeley shimmered with its campanile ringing against the sky would have been the crystalline skyline of Niteroi. Benjamin smiled. The bridge linked the two countries of his life.

Amy reached the parapet and leaned beside him, inhaling the fresh breeze.

"You're tired, sit down," she ordered. But he waved her off.

"Who's tired? I know what's good for me!" he barked. The blood returned to his face and he smiled and pointed out the sights he recognized from a 1936 travel poster. *Oakland, Produce Terminal of the Pacific.* Fog was spiked on the ugly radio antenna on Twin Peaks. But it was clear as crystal from Yerba Buena Island to the emerald green slopes of Marin. When he pointed toward Sausalito he began to tell her about the houseboat, but from here he could see the million dollar condominiums that priced him out of the market. He would probably end up in a retirement hotel in the fog zone. But he boasted he'd find a place with a view and they'd barbeque on the roof and watch the same sunset the tycoons toasted from the

Top of the Mark. He'd own San Francisco like the humble favela dwellers owned Rio.

It stabbed Amy to hear him talk like this. He might be ready to live on his own but she wasn't. She pulled an article from the *Bay Guardian* out of her coat pocket. It was about alternative housing in San Francisco. The map showed a zone dubbed the Sunbelt, behind the foggy Twin Peaks, and a Latino barrio called the Mission. Maybe she could share an apartment there with Benjamin so he could hang out in cafes along Mission Street. She closed the map. Let him talk; she'd have a better chance to find a place without his knowing.

"You'll drop by sometimes?" he said.

"I don't want to talk about it."

"Then you won't come?"

"Of course I will, Benjamin. You don't have to ask that."

"Not yet." He tousled her hair. But he knew how people get isolated in cities. And someday she'd have a beau. But she'd come for a while, he reassured himself, and he'd find new friends. It was easier now, after opening up to her; he was finding people everywhere. His feelings balled up. He pulled his hand from Amy's tangled hair.

"So what are you going to do?" he said. "It's almost three-thirty. So far, all I've heard is which jobs you don't want, and which ones don't want you. You've gotten talked into rejection and recession and depression -- all the shuns. Quit making compromises and tell me: What is the perfect job?" He realized he'd reverted back to his preaching tone and halted himself.

"Yeah, the perfect job in an hour and a half," Amy laughed bitterly. "At this point I'd take anything."

"Then you'll get nothing!" Lightning seemed to flash from his eyes. He paced the turret. How could he show her? He leaped behind Amy and thrust his hands over her eyes and turned her to face the bay. She bridled, but he thundered, "If you could have any job in the world, what would you wish for?"

Amy struggled beneath his hands. He was stronger than she had thought. She remembered when she'd first met him, how he'd closed his eyes when he talked of his dreams. Benjamin didn't open them until they arrived in Iowa City. Now he was trying to get her to give herself to her dreams. "Let go!"

"What do you see?" he demanded, holding the struggling woman. It hurt him to do this to her, but she must dream blindly if she was to seek the ultimate.

Images floated up behind Amy's eyelids. They seemed so close, so accessible. Without being able to describe it, she saw what she wanted in San Francisco. She glimpsed why Benjamin closed his eyes -- dreams were so vulnerable. She knew how easily they could turn to delusions. But she stopped struggling and accepted the vision.

"Now go find it," he whispered, pulling his hands away. Amy blinked, feeling light and dizzy. The bay was pale compared to her dream.

Benjamin turned away. After she'd stopped struggling and he felt her relax, a load of anxiety fell off him. He had no right to do this, only affection. Benjamin stiffened before the approaching fog. He was tired; he'd conjure his dream later. He felt his feet being guided down the stairs, winding closer and closer to the center of the tower in the waning afternoon. The descent brought him backward in time to the Great Depression portrayed in the mural. He nearly tripped on the last stair. But Amy descended sure-footedly in the darkness.

They caught a cab, blurring past sophisticates to the dreary State Employment Bureau near the Civic Center. They peered through the doors at the long lines, the tiny interview cubicles, the bent backs of petitioners filling out forms, and the impassive faces of state employees. On a bulletin board, they read the listings: "Op Avail Med Asst 2 yrs exp pt. time." The recession spirit screamed at Amy and Benjamin from every corner of the room. Amy had felt this futility in the people applying at the museum, but this office seemed like the propagation point of the recession.

Benjamin examined the machinery of social welfare that America had constructed to prevent another depression, a levee of paperwork and bureaucracy thrown up against the flood of jobless Americans. He didn't know if it was more oppressive than the catastrophic rising and falling of the business cycle. He only knew that Amy would not get a job here today. During the Great Depression, he had been in the business of giving hundreds of people jobs of last resort, and now he was powerless to find even one.

At four o'clock -- the ominous roar of rush hour -- Benjamin dragged Amy across Market Street and headed through the streets of flophouses and bars where they had started the day. Amy recognized the desolate district south of Market Street.

"Are we going back to the bus station?"

"No!" he shouted. "We're going to get some Jonathan apples." He shook his head at her protests and quickened his pace. Benjamin had seen an employment agency that morning, the sign had been blotted out by the glow of oranges, but now he vaguely remembered seeing a Day Laborers Wanted sign. It wasn't the kind of place he wanted to take her, but now there was no choice. Benjamin reached the excavation and retraced his steps, crossing through derelict business areas that had been burned by arsonists, ducking through alleys where flower brokers once sold their colorful wares, passing modern murals painted on the scaling brick walls of defunct produce warehouses. You couldn't teach an old dog new tricks. When things got rough, Benjamin always homed to fruit.

They could paint murals of rainbows to cheer up the walls, but he would always revel in the rusty light cracking through commercial streets at sunrise. It was the same in any city in America, the out-of-work men stood warming their hands on tin can fires and waiting for a crate of fruit to hawk downtown. Benjamin reached the corner and stopped. The orange vendor was gone. But the A-1 Employment Agency, refurbished in the 1950s with fluorescent lights, venetian blinds, and brown folding chairs, stood on the corner.

In how many agencies like this had he recruited vendors in New York? He took off his hat and opened the glass door, the pane with the name painted in red and white letters rattling in the frame. He ushered Amy in. A bell jingled, but no one looked up.

A-1 had changed little since the Depression, preserving the name and location only because there was no reason to alter them, and surviving in the derelict neighborhood by providing cheap labor for demolition and rehab projects, as it had once procured manpower for the farmer's market and warehouses. He could smell the musky mix of smoke and sweat, picture the fan and the rusty filing cabinets, before he entered. Half a dozen people, some writing on forms perched on the arms of scarred school desks, were scattered in front of the counter where Mr. Meyer, the job broker, appraised the applicants.

Mr. Meyer was a bald, bowling pin of a man in his late sixties who chewed a cigar and wore a necktie yanked out of his collar. He was a keen judge of people and could match jobs to workers with the mastery of a matchmaker. The clients he divided into two groups.

The hopeless lost who had been searching for jobs for so long they only knew how to be refused and agonized over each question on the application form as a kind of penance for the sin of unemployment. And the hopeless found, who were on the unemployment benefit roles and had to go through the motions of appearing to look for a job to impress their welfare counselors. At six a.m., the serious job seekers turned up at A-1, but in the afternoon the jobless leisure class took up his time.

When Benjamin and Amy entered, Meyer looked up and saw a couple that confounded his categories. Unlike the state job computer that would have taken their punch cards and spat them out for not being California residents, he glanced at Benjamin's flowered tie and Amy's stark eyes and decided to give them two minutes of his time.

"Sorry, we're closed. Come back tomorrow." He said for openers. Throwing out his standard line to test their spunk.

Amy's face fell, but Benjamin had sized up the employment agent from his own repertoire of con artists and threw back, "That's too bad. I wanted to give you my business. Whenever I come into town I like to use A-1 for hiring."

"Oh, you've placed jobs with A-1 before?" asked Meyer, his interest piqued.

"Hundreds," Benjamin boasted, slamming down his palm on the counter to punctuate his point. He enjoyed sparring again. It made him feel almost thirty-nine. He picked up his stinging palm and smiled.

Now that Meyer was interested in getting his business, Benjamin maneuvered the conversation the other way. He didn't want to get pushed into revealing that he had done a lot of hiring -- in 1933.

"Tell me, how big is your stable of artists?" he ventured.

"What business did you say you were in?"

"I didn't."

"But you need artists?"

"You didn't answer my question."

"Small." Meyer meant A-1's non-existent file. Long ago, he had refused to deal with the swarm of unemployable artistes that had descended on San Francisco like locusts.

"How small?"

"Small. They're in great demand. I can't list them fast enough." Meyer lied like a fox.

"Why? Where do artists work?" Benjamin asked, hoping to get a lead for Amy.

Meyer smiled, deducing that the old fart wanted information without paying a commission. To throw him off, he shouted the least likely place he could think of to find artists, at least judging by the disasters he'd seen painted on the walls in the neighborhood. "At the rehab projects," he shouted. "They're taking up all the artists. You know, painting those god-awful murals."

"Murals!" Amy cried, coming to life. She closed her eyes and the images floated up again. When Benjamin had covered her eyes on the parapet, mural painting was what she'd envisioned. She didn't hear the two men talking. She didn't hear Meyer shout he had no listings, or hear Benjamin roar he wasn't offering any. She clenched her eyes and felt the incredible joy of this impossible chain of disappointments leading to...

"It's perfect, perfect!" she yelled with such enthusiasm that two passersby stopped arguing outside. "It's just what I dreamed of, Benjamin. I'll work outside, learn mural painting!" And she gushed on, oblivious to the embarrassing scene she was creating by showing her intimate wish to the whole employment office, with her eyes closed --like a fool, or an American dreamer? -- Benjamin didn't know which. He watched Meyer gaze at Amy, throwing off her fireworks like the 4th of July for a job he hadn't offered.

There was something so embarrassing in her optimism that the job broker cringed, but he couldn't take his eyes off her, couldn't bring himself to interrupt. Meyer had become so accustomed to saying no, hearing no, watching people take no for an answer, that Amy's display felt like a cool summer rain, washing away the cynicism, making him smile at the spectacle of a person who needed a job and still dared to dream.

Meyer shook his head, convincing himself it was impossible to find her one. Cursing, he picked up the phone and called his friend. "Can she paint signs?" he asked Benjamin.

"Of course! She's an artist. She can paint anything," Benjamin shouted into the horn. He stared at Amy's irrepressible attractiveness. Her talk would have sounded like painful delusion in him, but that was because he was old.

Benjamin shut his eyes as Amy opened hers.

"I can't promise you anything, but you've got a job tryout at Mission Sign Company," Meyer announced. "You'll like the boss, Alvey. You know those old-time painted billboards? He's a master of the art. Maybe he'll show you a secret or two when you're out hanging billboards. He smiled like he'd earned a million dollars, until the phone rang and another client started berating him. "Here's the address. Show up at eight tomorrow," he told Amy.

Amy took the piece of paper. Benjamin turned away. Then Amy threw herself into his arms and he crushed her to him and they wheeled around and around, hugging each other as the job applicants looked up from their forms. Amy pressed her lips against Benjamin's cheek, but her thanks were drowned out by the gush of blood in his ears as he whirled, nearly lifting her off the ground. "How about that -- a job! A job!" So much energy coursed through her, he believed he was grasping life itself. The current ran through him like an electric shock, then she shot out of his arms toward the door, and he leaned against the counter, weak but overjoyed. While the fish were biting, he wanted to throw in a line for himself.

"Let's celebrate!" he boomed. "Go get some oysters and pink champagne. I'm going to check out the opportunities."

She smiled at his choice of delicacies and slipped through the door. It was twilight, nearly five o'clock, and the thought struck her that Benjamin wouldn't have time to look tonight. But she turned back and saw him leaning on the counter with his shoulders plumped up like an eagle, his head turned at a rakish angle, and his moustache drawn like a curtain to his ears, rippling as he talked to Mr. Meyer, and she thought Benjamin would make time. She wanted something extra for their feast. She turned the corner and lit out in the night, looking for fresh oysters.

"Special recession hours-- We'll stay open till six o'clock tonight!" Meyer bragged to Benjamin. But when he heard Benjamin wanted to check job listings on the Rolodex file, his enthusiasm cooled to realism. He saw Benjamin's chances for what they were -- a man past retirement age in a threadbare suit. But he gave him the application form to list himself with the agency. "Sit down and fill it out. Don't overdo the biographic details," he joked.

Benjamin smiled. He had decided to do just that.

Benjamin eased himself into a seat. He had never been so tired. Running from the orange vendor to the art museum to the trolley to Coit Tower to the Employment Bureau, dodging desperation, recession, depression, and gravity. A force at the center of the Earth caught him, pulling him into this chair. He wavered for a moment, dislocated, looking for Amy, and then he remembered she had gone out searching for party provisions.

He smiled, charged by the energy that coursed from her. She had found herself a job; everything lay before her! He felt himself running through the streets in her body, passing new prospects, veering through mysterious districts, winding out of back streets into the heart of a new town. Benjamin felt dizzy again. He gripped the armrest and knocked the application onto the floor.

He leaned over to pick it up, and gravity almost pulled him out of his chair. Blood came rushing into his ears and his vision blurred. But the sheet was white against the dirty linoleum and he snatched it up and leaned back, hoisting the walls up to their proper locations and shutting the din out of his ears. And suddenly he was sitting on the rocks by the sea, soaked and breathless after swimming out around the point in the riptides to drown his misery after Gisela died, and he felt the silent immobility of the rock, and the tenacious grip of the mollusks, and a white shell glimmered before him on the sand.

The top of the form asked for his critical information, and the bottom posed two simple questions: What work have you done? What job do you want? The standardized form chilled him. He felt the terrible helplessness of a job applicant. He had recruited men, but had never been recruited. It had taken nearly fifty years, but the circle had come 'round.

Bending under the weight of this terrible justice, he pulled out his pen. He felt lumpen as any proletarian, and a strange power crept into his fingers and traveled up his hand and arm, tensing his shoulders, tightening his chest. He looked around for the source, the way a tame bird set on a branch in the wind looks wonderingly for the force that pushes it. And then he realized the strength came from the pen. When defeated, he found solace in writing. Tears welled in his eyes as the old power to explain filled his being. He had divested himself of *Pearls*, but he could still write! The nib was dry after so much disuse, but he shook the pen and began to scratch across the page.

Benjamin East, 68 (He doubted Meyer would believe it, but why stop pretending now?), male, widower, Social Security number. Address: General delivery, San Francisco.

He set down the pen and felt light, the way he had when he started writing each new of *Pearls*. He grinned, enjoying the general delivery address and the blank beside Social Security. In this chapter of his life, he was starting out without much baggage.

The application asked for personal references. He laughed, his friends were all buried. He wrote:

Louie East, Dodger emeritus, Brooklyn, N.Y.

Amy McCaffrey, artist, Mission Sign Co., San Francisco.

For the third reference, he wondered whom to write down. He thought of using the cowboy and rifled his mind for other people he'd met on the trip, and then a gleam came in his eye and he scrawled:

Joshua Ratner, Writer, Iowa City, IA.

Benjamin's eyelids fluttered shut. He was riding on the bus one dawn or dusk, he couldn't remember which, feeling Amy's back against his side as she drew by the window. And he heard the cowboy cursing in the back and the baby wailing and the fellow named Jeffrey with the trivia book marking something on his map. And it didn't matter what he was saying to Amy, or what she was drawing, or Joshua was writing, or the bus was passing, only the bumping, wailing confluence of their lives streaming together down the American highway mattered. These people were his friends, a list of references scrawled across the country, people who'd speak up for him, as he would for them, because they had all shared that journey.

The chair bumped. A fellow in muddy construction boots had knocked into the leg, jarring Benjamin back into the employment office. It was five-fifteen; Amy had left only a quarter of an hour ago. He picked up the sheet and faced the first question. "Work experience." It was like asking him to write his autobiography! His right hand gnarled. He had written hundreds of pages in *Pearls* and still had not told his life story. How was he ever going to fit it in this two-inch space? Then he read the words in parenthesis: "List last job first."

That simplified things. Gave a format. Something he never had with *Pearls*.

Relieved, Benjamin set pen to paper. But in his mind, he was paddling upriver to reach Gisela, only to find she had miscarried. How many things in his life had he reached too late?

Benjamin lifted the pen. In the space, he had written a list:

Writer
Manufacturer of refrigerators
Import-export business
Uranium prospector
Crystal miner
Apple salesman.

That was his work experience. That was his life.

It seemed so short. Then his eye roved up and down and he thought: 'At least I didn't repeat myself.' Crystal mining led to uranium prospecting, and that was perhaps the great mistake of his life, when he had tried to take his experience with crystal into a jungle where he didn't belong. He was past looking for mistakes and turning points. Each stage was an attempt at progress, at betterment, maybe with the exception of import-export, when he was living the good life in Copacabana. That period had been the happiest of his marriage. The refrigerator factory was his greatest effort of will, and it had ended up as his greatest financial loss. His wedding and Gisela's death, the happiest and most painful moments, were un-recorded. Why should they be? Benjamin half-smiled. The first and last entries pleased him the most. Selling apples was his greatest accomplishment. Writing was the highest goal he had strived for. Between the aspiration and the accomplishment sprang his spirit -- the vitality that was his special gift. Sheer energy had taken him from apples to crystal to uranium to imported Cadillacs to gas refrigerators to *Pearls*, from New York to Brazil to California, without looking back with regret, without looking ahead with fear. Benjamin looked at the list and saw the bottom entry returning to the top. His experi-ence from the apple business had helped Amy get a job. He felt his life vindicated by this detail that jumped like a fish and expanded to encompass Amy and Benjamin in a widening circle. Benjamin looked up, expecting Amy to burst through the door any moment, and his lungs swelled and his heart pounded and his body stretched to encompass the room, break down the walls, sweep out into San Francisco, sail across America, touch Brazil!

But the hiring hall was empty. It was five-thirty and the disgruntled applicants had handed in their forms and disappeared into the dark, a migration of empty-handed humans wandering on a road that connected them to the migrations of emigrants from Europe, the lines of jobless in the Depression -- the circle of his life joining the circles of his time, leaving the human condition unaltered. Amy had gone, he knew, not confusing her imminent return for a return of their relationship in Moab.

Benjamin turned away from the door and faced the second question. "Job preference." A cramp stabbed his right arm and spread like a shot of cane liquor through his neck and shoulder, crabbing his hand until he could barely hold the pen. But though his vision blurred, he was able to read the question. He knew the fever had left him weakened and he had overdone it today. He knew unconsciously what was happening to him, but he wanted to answer the question about his future before being dragged into it.

Benjamin clutched the scarred desk Meyer had bought when they were remodeling the schools. Yes, if he had a job preference, it would be teaching. But first, he'd have to go back to school, get a degree. His pen hovered over the space. Teaching-- was that the job he really wanted? Knowledge was always like going back to square one -- asking one question led to all the others. And ultimately, he wasn't a man of questions or even answers -- but of acts. He nodded imperceptibly. In his life, he'd always preferred to do rather than to contemplate. He jumped into an experience and only considered how to get out when he started to sink in above his head. Brazil had been the biggest leap, swallowing up more than half his life, and it had taken quite nearly all his brains to find a path out. But when all was said and done, his book mattered less than the fact that it had propelled him back into America. Animals, minerals, fruit, and machines were only stepping stones to--

Where is Amy? What's keeping her?

He tried to lift his head and see through the window. His eyes closed, blindfolded by longing. Someone was chewing gum. He smelled the Acai berries that grew by the Rio Negro on his quest for Amazonian riches: the fateful journey to a miscarriage.

Ai, Gisela! He saw her accusing gaze when he returned from the jungle, too late. "Por que me abandonou?" *Why did you abandon me?* Yet she had forgiven him. Over thirty-six years of marriage, he'd remained a mystery to her and she to him, and that was the bond that had kept them together. He remembered Gisela's look of wonder and desire when he first kissed her at the Carnival ball at the Teatro Municipal. He had fallen in love with Gisela and with Brazil at the same moment, yet was slow to understand that his childless wife would become jealous of his passion for the Brazilian Dream. Still, Gisela had chosen him. Why? Because he promised to take her away from her sheltered life; or, because she knew he'd be lost without her? He would never know; it was her secret, strewn with her ashes over Corcovado.

"Meu Benjaminho.' Her voice calling him burst the charged storm clouds like a summer downpour.

The pen trembled. He crimped his elbow to his ribs. It felt like a freight train had slammed into his chest, its cargo of fruit flying everywhere, obliterating the logic and the sense of the words, and he was left tumbling through space with bushels of smashed pulp.

He straightened the pen. No, he wasn't ready to quit yet. The final riddle had been posed for him in the form of the blank space on the questionnaire.

But what was the question?

He'd forgotten. Or maybe he'd never known. Was that why his book had wandered off? It didn't matter. It had brought him to Amy. He gripped the pen. He had always known what he was looking for. Only he had gotten lost somewhere in the search. It shimmered on the page, white as a pearl, winding as a river, rich as a garden, but stripped of its guises.

He reached for it.

CHAPTER 28

B uoyantly balancing a bottle of $2.99 champagne and a carton of oysters, Amy reached A-1 five minutes before closing. She was sorry she was late, but on a bulletin board at the grocery she'd found a lead to an apartment. She glanced through the blinds into the fluorescent room and saw Benjamin dozing on a brown folding chair, ignored by the last job applicants. She was struck by déjà vu -- Benjamin dozing in the Washington depot, wearing the same flowered necktie, the same suit, the same Panama hat with Zazza's brilliant feather in its band. Everything that had happened to them rushed over her.

She sailed through the door, ringing the bell, holding out her gift. She hesitated. Benjamin still looked like he was dozing -- but his right hand crumpled the paper in a distorted grip. His head hung forward. His face was a blank mask. Two men scribbled nearby, oblivious.

"Benjamin, I think I found us an apart--" His eyes rolled open and stared straight through her. "Benjamin!" she cried, shaking him. A faint labored breathing rattled his throat. She tore open his collar, pulled him onto the floor, and started to breathe into his mouth. His tongue blocked his throat.

Meyer told her not to worry. San Francisco had the top emergency medics in the Bay Area. But it took nearly twenty minutes for an ambulance to come. The siren whined and they loaded Benjamin on a stretcher and the ambulance crossed Market Street, wreathed in fog, and sped toward San Francisco General Hospital, the opposite direction than they had taken that morning.

They halted at the emergency entrance. Benjamin was wheeled between automatic doors and pushed down a corridor into a cardiac unit, where he disappeared in a netherworld of white coats and beeping machines.

An admissions clerk wanted Benjamin's insurance number.

Amy pulled out his wallet and gave her the first ID card she found, his Brazilian Carteira de Identidade.

"He an illegal alien?"

"He's American!" She opened his passport: The dark, handsome Benjamin East gazed into the ineluctable future. "He was going to get it renewed tomorrow."

* * *

After waiting forty-five minutes, Amy stole down to the Intensive Care Unit. Through a maze of curtains, she saw a disembodied head like a bruised fruit, with tubes sticking in and out of the mouth and nostrils. A heart-lung machine hummed, a white blip flashed on a green screen.

The waiting room was full. TV screaming like a mad Cyclops. She stared at the crumpled resume Benjamin had filled out. The list of jobs seemed terse, incomplete. A seismic ink mark showed the heart attack. He'd kept on writing, the letters growing cribbed. The last word was unfinished. She looked at the space he'd left blank.

At 2:30, a resident opened the door and asked her to sign a release form for the deceased. "Are you his daughter?"

She shook her head. "He has a brother, Louie, in New York."

"Will you inform him?"

* * *

Amy found the yellow scrap of paper where Benjamin had scrawled Louie's phone number. She shut her eyes. The long distance phone rang off the hook. It was 5 a.m. in New York. Finally, somebody snatched up the receiver and an unmistakable voice shouted, "Hullo?" His next words were drowned out by squawking in the background.

"Louie, this is Amy," she stammered.

"You know what time it is?" he asked, and then shouted, "shut up Zazza!"

The squawking died down.

"I'm sorry to disturb you, but Benjamin -- "

"What does he want, money?" Louie seemed to gloat, triumphant. "Tell him I'll wire him a plane ticket home. But that's it."

"No." She gouged her nails into her wrist. "He died this morning."

"What?" A beat of stunned silence from his end was followed by "Oomph." As if a Louisville Slugger bat had slammed into his solar plexus. She berated herself, why did I tell him so bluntly? The screeching bird rendered his glottal cries into heart-rending gibberish. Amy clung to the armored phone cord, as she'd once clutched Benjamin's flowered tie and swung into the taxi. "Take me to New York!"

"How?" Louie croaked.

"A heart attack." She tried to cushion the blow. "I don't think he suffered."

"Were you two having...?"

"No!" she cried, affronted. "He was filling out a job application."

"That cheat!" Louie mumbled. "He beat me again. Stormed out of life like he'd bawled into it -- first."

It was a poor connection and she couldn't make out what he was saying. "What?"

"He called and told me he wasn't exactly in the pink of health. But I thought he was just trying to make me feel sorry for him." She heard Lou's gravelly voice subside. "He had no right."

"It was my fault." An invisible hand clutched her throat. "I--"

"You gave him the time of his life!" Lou said, stifling a cough. "My brother, that lousy Don Juan, called and told me. He made me jealous."

She crossed her arms over her breasts, feeling exposed. Keep your dirty thoughts to yourself. But she owed it to Benjamin to put up with his brother's failings. They were lifelong rivals, and now he was alone. Grief-stricken.

"I want him back in New York," Lou said. "He named this town and this is where he belongs. I'll authorize the papers--" and he was seized with a coughing fit.

She imagined him shaking his fist at an invisible umpire. "He left some money," Amy said. "I'll use it to pay the hospital and..."

"No, Ben said he was going to give you a surprise, a nest egg to get you started out there."

"He didn't have enough money to..."

"When did money make a difference to Benjamin?"

She pressed her head against the holes in the sound-proof booth. "Thanks, it'll help," she said. "What should I do with his suitcase?"

"Send it to me," he said. "But I don't want that book. Throw it in the trash."

There was an awkward silence.

"Benjamin wanted you to come out and stay with him," Amy said. "He missed your fights."

"Really? I guess I may one day. Look, if you ever come to New York, there's a room open."

"I might take you up on it." She heard squawking in the background.

"Shut yer beak!' Louie yelled. "This damn parrot arrived yesterday. I don't know the whole story, but apparently my brother tried to smuggle it in, and it was put in quarantine. Ben gave them my address and then skipped out. The delivery boy demanded two hundred and fifty clams C.O.D., payable to Uncle Sam. Like a fool, I paid! Goddamn parrot is driving me crazy!" Louie roared. "It shits all over the place. Bites the hand that feeds it, just like my brother. I got no room for it."

"Oh, dear." She pictured the apartment she'd planned to share with Benjamin, and couldn't bear the emptiness. "I'll take care of it."

"That's a kind offer, young lady. I'll even pay for shipping. Anything to get it off my hands."

She promised to send him her address as soon as she had one. There was nothing left to say.

* * *

Lou stood with the dead phone in one hand and the oxygen mask in the other. He stifled the urge to hurl Zazza out the window, bomb Brooklyn with his grief. But he covered the cage with a blanket, opened the window, and leaned his head against the sash. The water towers were in shadow; beyond the rooftops, shot with beams of gold, across the East River, rose the towers of Manhattan. He remembered when Benjamin's office was on the 36th floor of the Empire State Building. They'd fought over a check at the Copa, wrestling to prove who was the most successful, and the table went over, silver and crystal crashing -- and Benjamin announced he was going to South America. Now Lou shivered in the draft, wondering if their rivalry had pushed his brother out of New York, out of America, into that wild blue yonder of Brazil from which he returned only once, briefly, a broken man pontificating on the jewelry of life.

The sun flew behind a cloud. He watched a bus pick up a lone rider then rush on in a trail of smoke, leaving the street deserted. The towers turned grey, indecipherable as tombstones. A siren wailed somewhere, through the streets of the city that had nearly gone broke. And what did the idiots on Madison Avenue do to try to resurrect it? They dredged up the Big Apple myth and painted it five stories high above Times Square, while the man who'd been responsible for hawking the apples pounded the streets, unable to even sell his story.

Towers! Tombstones! Lou's eyes blurred with tears of rage. Maybe Benjamin was right after all, New York was just the tallest, most crowded cemetery in the world. But something on the periphery tugged Lou's eye to the street. A waiter toted a red and blue umbrella onto the sidewalk, setting up an outdoor cafe. And last week, heading to City Hall to complain about his electric bill, he'd passed an old warehouse district. The whole area had been turned into restaurants and shops. Sexy girls in stiletto heels swung bags with the Big Apple on their hips. Red kisses.

Maybe something was happening in New York. The news wasn't so gloomy lately. The TV said out west in the Sunbelt the construction industry was dead, but here in New York there were skyscrapers going up. And in the Daily News he'd read, "A giant apple sculpture will be erected in Times Square to launch the 'Save the Big Apple' campaign." Did Benjamin East have anything to do with it? Of course not. But still the Big Apple meant something.

Lou thrust his head out the window. The cafe table was set up and there were people sitting out there at 8 a.m. having coffee and danishes. Street vendors. Only a madman or a dreamer could have predicted it. Benjamin hadn't. He'd been blinded by his own rejection, couldn't see the sidewalk vendors were taking up his tradition. He'd stormed out of the city because nobody gave him credit. Funny, because when he was in his prime he didn't give a damn for fame. Ran out of restaurants when people recognized him.

And Lou saw, clear as day, his brother striding out of the Copa nightclub and charging down 5th Avenue like a bull, past Tiffany's, marching straight to the travel agent in Rockefeller Plaza and ordering a ticket for the most primitive place in the hemisphere, Brazil.

Lou shook his fist at the Latino waiter -- he was probably Puerto Rican, not Brazilian, but they all acted the same -- and shouted "Fools!" at the sidewalk customers.

Well, he'd show Benjamin for heading off into the wilderness and playing Johnny Appleseed. He'd plant his body where it belonged, in the family plot in Brooklyn, under a granite stone that wouldn't let him skip off to any more adventures. And instead of a tablet or a Star of David, he'd commission a starving artist -- they were plentiful nowadays -- to carve an apple inscribed, "Benjamin East, the Big Apple." The waiter saw an old man gesticulating from high up in the building and waved back with a smile, showing a piano keyboard of white teeth. Louie waved back, struck by a sudden craving for grapefruit. Then, disgusted, he slammed the window and fired up a stogie, scattering ashes on the funnies.

CHAPTER 29

A my made all the arrangements and went back to the Greyhound station to pick up Benjamin's suitcase. The placid waters of the bay and the necklaces of lights on the bridges seemed quarried from a world that knew no pain. She understood how Benjamin found solace in minerals. But when she opened the locker, a gaping hole stared back at her. Here was all that was left. Battered vessel of his dreams.

She opened the valise, smelling the faint odor of Benjamin's cologne.

The manuscript fell out with a thump. What should she do with it? Maybe Louie was right, toss it in the trash.

She began to read a page and halted, hearing Benjamin's voice caressing the words, telling the story about the human and the jewel. Why had he thrown away Aquamarine? Benjamin must have felt he'd thrown away his life. She was holding all that was left of it and she had no idea of what to do with it. Then she remembered the crumpled job application. She pulled it out and smoothed it out and stuck it at the end of the manuscript.

Her eye fell on the list of references. Benjamin had written Joshua's name. Bitterly, she went to a booth and placed a collect call to Iowa City.

Joshua stood naked amid the papers erupted from his typewriter on another all-night writing binge. He stuttered yes, Operator, he'd take the call, and felt his adrenaline rise. "Amy, it's incredible, I was just thinking about you the other day. Did you find Benjamin?" Before she could answer, he bowled on, "You know that weirdo named Jeffrey, with a face like a runny egg, on the bus? He was collecting trivia. Well, by chance, I saw him on the tube. He was a contestant on a quiz show. The MC thrust the mic in his face and asked, 'How did the Big Apple get its name?'"

"Then Jeffrey licked his lips and said, 'This old coot sold apples to the ex-millionaires on the street corners of New York during the Depression. They named the Big Apple after him.'"

"Was it the right answer?" Amy held her breath.

"Sorry. Apparently the Big Apple is race-track slang from the Twenties."

"He's gone."

Silence.

"I gotta go," she said.

"Wait! I was thinking that fable about the grain of sand becoming a pearl might work for a children's book, if somebody illustrates it."

She closed her eyes, conjuring up Sandy and the Human. Her fingers twitched to hold, once again, the pastels Benjamin had picked up off the floor in the DC bus depot.

She said goodbye and hung up and walked toward the glass doors. She needed a few moments to herself.

It was nearly six and the sun was coming up. The sky was raw, red. Instead of being relieved, the total emptiness of the dawn swallowed her. This was the first dawn Benjamin would not see. His hat, which had been left on the floor of A-1, now hung in wisps of cloud in the east, Zazza's flight feather, a streak of orange light. Amy struggled with everything that was in her not to run away, to face this day. And then she remembered she had a job. She held onto that straw as the city began to awake, the hills coming alive with the routine of daily life, the avenues and streets growing crowded.

Amy bought a paper and hid in a back booth at Lori's Diner, remembering how he had handed her the want ads. "Welcome to the real world." Now it had taken him from her, without even leaving an obituary.

She opened Benjamin's crocodile pouch and discovered his Brazilian gemstones: topaz, emerald, watermelon tourmaline and a pearl. She picked up Gisela's engagement ring. Aquamarine! It was marred by an occlusion, like their marriage, but still shone.

Tears welled up in her eyes, blurring her vision. Unable to contain her grief, she broke down and cried, making loud convulsive gasps.

Then it passed like the thundersnow. She put the ring and gemstones back in the pouch and gulped down black coffee. Caffeine restored her courage. She opened Benjamin's wallet and went through it 'til she came to a snapshot of Gisela sunning on the beach, her gorgeous body straining a white swimsuit, her tanned skin glistening with coconut oil. The picture he carried of her, eternally young and beautiful. Gisela had died and Benjamin had survived to meet Amy, and now she had survived him. The world went 'round and 'round, like the stairs up Coit Tower, and you only caught a glimpse of meaning when you closed your eyes.

Under the counter, she counted the crumpled bills in his wallet. It wasn't a pittance. There were twelve hundreds, one fifty, assorted tens, fives, and ones, and one thousand cruzeiros. Nearly thirteen hundred bucks, she totaled up. The number rang a bell. Then she remembered him running out of the Land Office in Moab, shouting, "The Garden of Eden exists, but I owe $1,300 in back taxes!"

The symmetry of his life struck her; after all his struggles, he only possessed what he owed in taxes for his dream. She thought her heart would burst, but she closed her eyes and the garden floated up.

It was seven a.m. Amy went into the ladies room and washed her eyes with cold water, splashed some color into her sunken cheeks, and brushed some luster back into her hair. Her face had grown thinner and grey shadows hung below her eyes, but the lines had disappeared from her forehead and appeared around the corners of her mouth. They were smile lines. For a month, she had smiled almost constantly without knowing it. She had to dry her cheeks and bite into a crisp apple before showing up at Mission Sign Co.

She packed up her things and hurried out onto streets ringing with morning traffic. It was only seven-thirty, but she wanted to be early for her new life.

Crossing Market Street, she clasped Benjamin's wallet deep inside of her coat pocket. She knew what she was going to do with that money. She was going to pay the back taxes on the orchard in Moab and somehow keep its name. And no matter how badly things went with her art, or how confusing her life got, there would always be a place she could go to eat a snow apple and taste the infinite possibilities.

THE STORY BEHIND THE NOVEL
&
ACKNOWLEDGMENTS

As a young writer, I was fascinated by a larger-than-life fictional character, Benjamin East. He was an early success in New York in the Depression, but lost everything in Brazil and sought a comeback in America. I wrote the first draft in my early thirties, but couldn't support my family on fiction. So I got a job as an editorial writer and put the manuscript in a box. My journalism career took off. The novel stayed in the box for over thirty years.

Flash forward to 2012. I'm now in my sixties, nearly Benjamin East's age, and have tasted success and failure. In a blue mood, I dust off the manuscript. I'm swept away by the spirit of Benjamin East. Yet the first draft has flaws. So the two Jonathans — the young novelist, and the seasoned author — collaborate to bring the novel to fruition

This miracle could not have happened without the intercession of my literary angels.

Daniel Tucker urged me to open the box releasing Benjamin East. "It's a poignant story of the consequences of a man's choices on the trajectory of his life," he wrote. "It is your story, and it is the story of everyman who reaches our stage of life."

Michele Gibson read the manuscript in three sittings. "You've got to publish this book." As publisher of Bright Lights Press, you fulfilled that promise. With my abiding gratitude.

Bill Tancer, my writing buddy, read the manuscript late into the night. "Beautiful novel, engaging. BRAVO." We helped each other make our books better.

Susannah Carlson took on the task of editing the novel. This arduous process she accomplished with wit and perspicacity, and she never gave up.

I asked City College of San Francisco for a star graphic design student. Yulia Zimmermann, a native of Ukraine, brought her enthusiasm and artistic talent to the project. She created the front and back covers. A parrot's feather in your cap!

I have so many people to thank along the way:

My mother, Betty, for encouraging me to be a writer. My father, Marshall, for holding me to high standards. My English teacher at Exeter, Mr. Tremallo, who gave a lonely boy from Denver an outlet to write. To my professors at Columbia: Michael Goldman, Stephen Marcus, and Steven Donadio. To poet Kenneth Koch, for the Cornell Woolrich Prize that enabled me to travel to South America.

To David, Lucette, and Benjamin Borwick, who took me into their home in Rio de Janeiro and introduced me to the magic of Brazil. Your spirits are a living legacy.

To Maggie Locke, who shared the journey from Brazil to San Diego, and whose book, *The Cliffs of Coosheen*, awaits publication.

To my children Madigan, Nick, Viva and Lincoln, and grandchildren Belle and Milo. You give meaning to my life beyond words.

To my wife Isabelle for her constant love and support from La Jolla, to Switzerland, to our home in Burlingame.

I dedicate this book to you all, and to generations of travelers who leave their homes and take the road to infinite possibilities.

May, 2015, Burlingame, California

ABOUT THE AUTHOR

Jonathan Freedman was raised in Colorado and edu-
cated at Columbia University, where he won the Cornell
Woolrich writing award for a novel. The prize money
allowed him to travel overland from Mexico to Bolivia,
across the Andes, into the Amazon, to become a foreign
correspondent in Brazil. His experiences would later in-
spire the creation of THE LAST BRAZIL of BENJAMIN
EAST.

His editorial series for *The San Diego Tribune* was in-
strumental in the passage of U.S. immigration reforms
that brought two million undocumented immigrants out
of hiding and onto the road to citizenship.

Jonathan was awarded a Pulitzer Prize for that work
in 1987. He is the author of books on poverty, education,
and social issues. He has taught writing at San Diego
State University, in inner-city public schools, and at
Riker's Island prison. He leads a writing workshop at
City College of San Francisco.

Jonathan lives in Burlingame, California with his wife
and children.